SMALL TOWN
NIGHTMARE

A gripping thriller full of mystery and suspense

ANNA WILLETT

THE
BOOK
FOLKS

Paperback edition published by

The Book Folks

London, 2018

ISBN 978-1-7200-7440-3

www.thebookfolks.com

For my beautiful daughters, Monica and Grace.

Chapter One

Despite the dip in temperature, the night skies were clear and freckled with stars. Tim finished peeing and followed the light from his phone back to the tent. Once inside, he rolled out his sleeping bag, smiling at the ponies galloping across the nylon cover. The one-man tent and girl's sleeping bag were a bargain at eighteen dollars *and* worth their weight in gold on cold nights. He'd also gone crazy and bought a battered copy of *How it Works – Volume 5* for fifty cents. It was the one book in the series he'd never read, so the probability of coming across a copy at a small town garage sale was somewhere in the range of eight thousand to one. Maths aside, Tim took the find as a good omen, not that he believed in such things. Still, spotting the out-of-date manual on a table littered with porcelain dog statues and Tupperware containers set his pulse racing.

He closed the book and shoved it in his pack. If his sister, Lucy, could see him now, camped illegally just outside a small town, she might not be impressed by his choice of lifestyle, something they'd agreed to leave out their infrequent chats. But she'd certainly have something to say about his living arrangements.

Tim pulled a dark woollen beanie out of his pack and stretched it over his head, dragging the edges down so his ears were covered. Fishing his small stash out of a rolled-up pair of socks buried at the bottom of the pack, he threw open the tent flap and shuffled outside.

Being alone and in the outdoors cleared his mind. He was still taking his pills, but the haze of hopelessness that had shadowed him since his mid-teens seemed to be blown away by the crisp air and stillness of the forest. He suffered from depression, but wasn't an idiot. Tim knew his brain wasn't really affected by smog and traffic, but the weight of the world filled the city streets in a way that pushed down on him until life seemed endless and without meaning.

He rolled a joint and lit it, sucking in the smoke and holding it in his lungs. "Oh yeah." He spoke to the moon, full and silvery, then let the smoke roll over his tongue and out into the night air.

Around him, the forest was quiet, only the infrequent hoots from a lone owl broke the silence. He'd have to head back in the morning, find a place to charge his phone, then make the journey home. Lucy would be thirty-three in a few days; her birthday was like a homing beacon, his signal to check in. Tim didn't mind making the trek; his only regret was leaving behind the wildness of living outdoors.

He was a tramp, a vagrant, any of the tags put on him fitted, but none of them mattered. After his last stint in Graylands Hospital, he had decided to stop trying to force his mind into suburbia and just be. Whether it was the miles of deserted coastline, the rugged bushland or the forest, as long as he could breathe and maybe score some weed, he was as close to happy as his brain would allow.

With the joint clamped between his lips, Tim pulled out his phone. Only a few bars left, but enough to send Lucy a message and use the torch until he found a visitors' centre in town. He fired off a text and attached a photo, noticing it was now ten p.m. She'd be asleep, getting her rest so she could get into work early in the morning. He couldn't help chuckling at how different they were. Lucy the journalist, always pushing for the next big story, and him… Tim's thoughts wavered. He wished he could be there for her more. Since their parents died, his sister had been a mother to him. His protector, always making time to attend his psych meetings, but in many ways Lucy was as lost as him. She needed someone. Someone that was strong enough for *her* to lean on.

He took one last drag then pinched off the lighted end of the joint. He'd stay longer this time, make an effort to make Lucy's birthday special. The twentieth of June was the anniversary of their parents' death, but maybe after all these years they could celebrate it as her day, without the pull of sorrow.

After stowing the small butt with his stash, Tim crawled back inside the tent and folded himself into the sleeping bag. Outside the tent came a crackling of twigs and the brush of leaves. Tim attributed the sounds to the usual nocturnal creatures moving around in the bush. He closed his eyes and fell into an easy sleep. Some time later, heavy boots landed at the entrance to the tent.

Chapter Two

Lucy pulled off the highway and lowered the window, letting the country air blow her hair back. It had been almost an hour and a half since she'd spotted a petrol station or shop and the need for caffeine was taking its toll. Not that her nerves needed heightening. Between the constant worry and frustration, she was about as awake as a woman could be without actually spinning in the driver's seat. No, for Lucy, caffeine acted as a depressant, lulling her racing mind.

Tim had been missing for six days and in that time Lucy had driven herself to the point of exhaustion and was still nowhere with the cops. The road narrowed and took a sharp turn to the left, opening out to a wide stretch flanked by a few signs offering locally grown fruit and the promise of fresh eggs.

"Jesus, I'd kill for a flat white and a greasy burger." Lucy tapped the steering wheel and shifted in her seat.

The lush growth on either side of the road reminded her of family holidays in the South, canoeing in a river somewhere near Dwellingup. She frowned. Or was it Preston? All she could remember for sure was the sweet smell of the forest and Timmy's chubby little face peeking out over the top of his life-jacket. Rather than making her smile, the memory set off a spike of anxiety that squeezed her chest until she felt her breath faltering.

"Okay. Enough." She spoke to the empty car. Taking her eyes off the road for a few seconds, Lucy switched on the radio.

When her gaze returned to the bitumen, something darted out of the trees and into the road. Lucy shrieked out a yelp of surprise and floored the brake. The tyres screeched and the front of the vehicle shuddered. As if flying, the car veered right in a sickening skid.

The whole incident lasted less than four seconds, but when the Saab came to a sudden halt, Lucy's arms were shaking like she'd spent ten minutes lifting weights. For some reason she couldn't peel her gaze off her hands and the way they were clamped on the wheel like white claws. And then the sound, a *humpf* as the vehicle began its skid, rang out in her mind. *I hit something.* The realisation, like a rapid descent in a speeding elevator, sent her stomach flipping into her throat.

Lucy shifted her stare off the wheel and onto the road. Before she had the chance to register the shape at the driver's window, something thumped the glass. Jumping and ducking left, Lucy let out a croaking scream.

"Are you okay?" The man at the window, a dark shaggy-haired silhouette, leaned close to the glass.

For an instant, with the sun at his back, Lucy thought it was Tim. At least that's how her jittering brain registered the shape. It took her less than a second to realise the man wasn't her brother but a scruffy-looking stranger.

Still reeling from the terrifying skid, Lucy managed to nod and open the door. "Yes." She didn't sound like herself. "I'm fine, thanks." As she tried to step out of the car she realised her seatbelt was still clipped.

"Are you sure?" The man stepped back as she exited the vehicle. "You look a bit shaken up."

Lucy rested her arm on the open door to keep herself steady. "I'm okay. You didn't have to stop." As she spoke it occurred to her that she didn't remember seeing another car. Then, glancing in both directions and not seeing another vehicle, she frowned.

"Well, I didn't." The man gave a half smile that lifted one corner of his mouth. "I wasn't driving, just walking."

With her nerves settling, Lucy took a second to survey the stranger. He had the look of a drifter, was maybe in his late thirties and too old to be a backpacker. She glanced back along the road, hoping to spot another car, but the clear afternoon sun shone on deserted bitumen.

As if sensing her discomfort, he took another step back, putting at least a metre and a half between them. His hair was dark and shaggy, flattened on one side like he'd been asleep. His clothes were creased, but expensive-looking with a dark wool jumper under a leather jacket. The black pack slung over his shoulder was also leather, creased and obviously well-used. He seemed calm and relaxed, giving no outward appearance of being drunk or high. Still, the whole situation felt a bit off.

"Um." Without coming right out and telling him to take a hike, Lucy could think of no way of moving the guy on without provoking a scene. "Well, it was still nice of you to come over and check on me, but really, I'm fine." She gave a chuckle that sounded nervous and completely lacking any humour.

The man shrugged. "No problem." He ran a hand over his bristly chin and turned his gaze on the bitumen. "The fox didn't do so well." He nodded towards the far side of the road.

"Oh no." The tremble that had started in her arms during the skid now travelled downwards, making her knees wobble as she followed the guy around the front of the car.

On the left, at the lip of a grassy embankment, lay a slumped form about the size of a smallish dog. As they drew closer, the sun splashed the creature's red fur with flecks of gold. Under different circumstances the effect would have been spectacular. But with the animal's front leg turned at a sickening angle and a splash of something pulpy and bloody spilling out of its rear end, the beauty of its fur made the carnage all the more obscene.

"Oh, Jesus." Lucy managed to turn away from the animal before a splatter of bile rushed out of her mouth.

Bent over on the side of the road, the smell of blood mixed with wet grass and the frantic cry of a flock of nearby cockatoos swirled around in her head until she thought the world might shift out from under her. Lucy groaned and gagged as another splash of vomit hit the bitumen. *What the hell is wrong with me?* As a journalist she'd seen worse, but something about seeing the wild creature reduced to blood and bone made her think of Tim.

"Here." The guy took hold of her elbow. "You need to sit."

Lucy allowed herself to be led to the car, sitting obediently in the passenger's side. She watched through watery eyes as the man grabbed the fox's tail and pulled the animal off the road. As he approached the car, Lucy noticed his size for the first time. Tall, maybe six feet, solid but not overly broad.

"Drink some water." He crouched in front of the open door and jerked his chin at the water bottle in the console.

Lucy nodded and picked up the water. Before drinking she pulled a tissue out of her pocket and wiped her mouth and nose. Her hands were shaking. More than shaking, they were juddering.

"I'm not normally like this." She took a sip of water, not sure why she was explaining herself to the stranger. "I've usually got it together." She tried for a smile, but her mouth couldn't quite pull it off.

"I'm Damon." His eyes were the colour of whiskey; he kept them trained on her face.

She hesitated, not sure if telling him her name was a good idea, but he *had* just watched her throw up her breakfast all over the road. What would it hurt to tell him her name? "Lucy."

He nodded. "Okay, Lucy. Do you want me to call someone?" He reached into his jacket and pulled out his phone.

"There's no... I mean, no. No need. I just need a minute." This time she managed a weak smile. "You've been really kind, but..." She let the words trail off. A few minutes ago she wanted him to get lost, but now she wasn't so sure. Something about his amber eyes, the steadiness in them, calmed her. "Do you need a lift?"

Picking up a hitchhiker wasn't the craziest thing she'd ever done, but it was up there. The real kicker was letting him drive. Lucy glanced over, watching Damon's casual posture, and wondered what a man who seemed so composed *and* normal was doing wandering the roads looking like he'd been sleeping rough.

"I was with a group of French kids." His voice startled her. As if reading her thoughts, he continued. "They gave me a lift from Busselton. Nice group, but too focused on partying. We were camping in the forest." He looked over and gave her a shrug. "When I woke up this morning they were gone. So there goes my fifty bucks petrol money."

"So, what now?" It was none of her business, but Lucy's journalism training kicked in. While asking questions she had control of the situation.

"Now," he began, drawing out the word, "I move on and look for work."

"Where's home?" It was the sort of question she asked in interviews. Get the subject thinking about their home and family and then they open up. After that you could get as personal as you wanted.

But Damon wouldn't be drawn. He shrugged and kept his eyes on the road. Lucy decided not to push it.

Besides, the guy's life story wasn't on her agenda. She was here to find Tim, not interview drifters. But as the thought crossed her mind it sparked an idea.

"You said you were with a group of French kids. No Australians in the mix?"

Damon frowned and shook his head. "Why? Are you looking for someone?"

* * *

The roadhouse was little more than a shack with a few picnic benches dotted to the left of the gravel parking lot. As the only occupant of the outside area, Lucy had no trouble spotting Damon. She approached the table and set down two takeaway cups of coffee. Before seating herself she pulled a brown paper bag out from under her arm and tossed it on the table.

"I got you a sausage roll." She swung her leg over the bench and sat opposite him.

"How much do I owe you?" He reached around to his back pocket.

Lucy waved a hand in front of her face. "Nothing. It's the least I can do after you were forced to watch me vomit my guts up back there."

He seemed about to protest, but then he nodded and picked up the bag. They sat in silence for a moment, Damon eating and Lucy blowing on her coffee. Before taking a sip, she pulled a packet of cigarettes out of her handbag and lit one. *Just one*, she told herself. After the incident with the fox, she thought she'd earned it.

"So, tell me about your brother?" Damon wiped his mouth with the back of his hand and picked up his cup.

Lucy took a drag on her cigarette then blew out a plume of smoke, watching the breeze grab the cloud and waft it into the air. She'd decided to tell Damon why she was in the south-west, hoping he might have seen her brother on his travels. One thing she'd learned from Tim was drifters liked to congregate – coming together and then flitting in different directions. Maybe if Damon was anything like her brother, they'd met up somewhere on the road. If not, maybe Damon had heard something from other travellers. She was grasping at straws, but with no real leads, it wouldn't hurt to ask the guy a few questions.

"Tim's been missing for four days." She frowned. "Four days that I know of. The last time I heard from him was three days before my birthday, so that puts his disappearance at anywhere from four to six days." She took another drag on the cigarette, noticing the way Damon's eyes changed colour in the sunlight. "The last message he sent me, he mentioned a place called Night Town."

For the first time Damon's steady gaze faltered and he looked towards the shed-sized aviary at the side of the picnic area. Lucy didn't know anything about the man, but her gut told her he'd heard of Night Town.

"Do you know it? Night Town, I mean. Have you been there?" Lucy waited. Her heart rate kicked up a notch. If Damon knew something, he might be the key to finding her brother.

When Damon turned back, his face was unreadable. "I've heard of the place, but never been there."

"Okay." Lucy nodded. "What have you heard?" She tossed the butt on the ground and crushed it.

"Small town. South of Margaret River." He rolled his shoulders. "An old place going back to the 1870s." He picked up his cup. "That's about it."

Lucy let out a sigh, but then thought of something else. "Sometimes Tim goes by the name McMurphy." She waved away Damon's confused look. "Don't ask, it's a long story. Anyway, maybe someone mentioned a guy named McMurphy?"

"Sorry." Damon took a sip of his coffee. "I wish I could help, but I've met a lot of people and no one's mentioned a Tim or a McMurphy."

"Oh well." Lucy tried to keep the disappointment out of her voice. It had been crazy to think it would be that easy. "Well, I'd better get going." She picked up the crushed butt and dropped it in her empty coffee cup.

"Do you want some company?" Damon turned on the bench and stood. "On the drive to Night Town, I mean." He gave her another of his lopsided smiles. "It's as good a place as any to look for work."

Lucy thought for a moment. Even though the guy didn't have any information, it might help to have someone to bounce a few theories off. Besides, she was sick of her own company.

"Well, I suppose if you were a serial killer I'd be dead by now." She almost laughed, but in light of Tim's disappearance, it didn't seem that funny anymore. She picked up her bag. "Why not."

* * *

The afternoon sun bathed the trees in warm light, softening the edges of the dense forest as it flanked both sides of the road. Feeling solid, if still a little shaken, Lucy drove. In the twenty minutes since leaving the road house, Damon had been silent. At one point Lucy glanced over wondering if the man had fallen asleep, only to find him watching the road as though he was mesmerised by the rush of bitumen.

"Why are you so sure?" Damon's question took her by surprise, but before she could ask for clarification, he continued. "How do you know your brother is missing? He could have just lost track of time or decided to take off somewhere. From what you've told me he's..." He paused, seeming to search for the right words. "...he lives by his own rules."

Lucy knew where he was going. It was the same response she'd gotten from the cops, but it surprised her coming from a man who was living the same sort of lifestyle as Tim.

"Yeah," she drew out the word. "He does live by his own rules." She glanced over at Damon. "But one of those rules is always coming home for my birthday. It's his rule, not mine." She wondered how much she should reveal. Her history was painful, and rehashing it for a stranger wouldn't really help. "It's complicated, but I know he wouldn't not show."

"Not unless something stopped him?" Damon asked, finishing her thought.

"Something or someone." As she spoke, they rounded a bend and the road tapered downwards. In the distance she could see a cluster of buildings dotted with patches of open fields and circled by forests. *Night Town.* The sight of it sent a ripple of gooseflesh running up her arms.

"You think he's down there somewhere?" Damon had turned in his seat and was studying her as if searching her reaction.

"It's the last place he mentioned before disappearing." She gripped the wheel tighter. "If he's there, I intend to find him."

Chapter Three

Entering Night Town, Lucy noticed a concentration of shops and businesses that circled the main street. A boulder sat in the middle of a roundabout that marked the town centre. A large black symbol rose from atop the giant stone. To Lucy, the tall artwork looked like a black key with a few strange bars criss-crossing the highest point. She made a mental note to return later and take a photo of the distinctive sculpture.

Once more, Damon seemed to be reading her mind. "Unusual, isn't it?" He nodded at the artwork as the Saab coasted along the main street.

"Mm. Where do you want me to let you out?" As much as she liked the company, it was time to do what she was here for.

"Anywhere on the main street will do."

When Lucy pulled over opposite a small supermarket, there was a moment when neither spoke. They'd been travelling together for only a few hours, including the time at the roadhouse, yet it felt strange to be parting and going their separate ways. Damon was attractive in a kind of dishevelled way and he was a good listener. In Lucy's experience, it was an unusual combination in a man.

"Thanks for the lift." Damon opened the passenger door and stepped out, his backpack dangling off his shoulder. Before closing it, he leaned in. "I hope you find your brother." The lopsided smile appeared again and Lucy found herself not wanting to let him go.

"Um. Look, why don't we meet up for dinner tonight." When Damon frowned it occurred to her that the man was probably broke. "My treat." She tried to sound confident, though she heard a note of desperation in her words.

"Sounds good." He jerked his chin to the pub on the corner. "I'll meet you in there, in the Royal Hotel at seven." He was just about to slam the door when he stopped. "I'll ask around and see if anyone knows anything about Tim. Who knows? Maybe between the both of us we can track him down."

Lucy felt a rush of gratitude towards the man. In the four days since Timmy went missing, Damon was the first person to take her seriously.

"Thanks."

As she pulled away, Lucy glanced in the rear-view mirror and saw Damon watching her departure. Before she looked away he raised a hand, giving her a casual wave.

* * *

Damon waited until Lucy's car disappeared around the corner. When he was sure the woman was out of sight, he crossed the road and headed for the side alley on the right of the small market. He tucked himself into the gloomy alcove and pulled out his phone.

The call took less than two minutes. When he was done, Damon slipped the phone in his pocket and opened the zip on the side of his pack. He pulled out a pocket-sized photograph. A young man with longish hair and a scruffy beanie gazed out from the image. Damon studied the picture for a moment, committing the man's image to memory. He didn't believe in coincidences, but meeting

14

Lucy had to be up there with the strangest chance meeting he'd ever encountered.

After a final glance, he put the photo back in his pack and ducked out of the alley. It was almost four p.m. He had a few stops to make before meeting Lucy for dinner. Walking slowly like he had all the time in the world, Damon headed back through the town centre and towards a motel he'd noticed as they drove in. He was looking forward to sleeping in a real bed later that night.

* * *

Lucy pulled into the parking lot behind the pub. It took her by surprise when Damon suggested they have dinner in the very place she'd booked a room. Just one of those things that meant nothing, no doubt. Still, enough to give her pause. But her usual cautious nature had to take a back seat to finding Tim and, so far, Damon was the only person interested in helping her. Not that he'd added much to the search, but the more people asking about her brother, the more likely they were to find answers.

Pulling a small red suitcase behind her, Lucy pushed open the glass door and entered the pub. The place was much as she'd expected: sticky carpet and thick walls. A race caller's harsh voice rang out from the TV on the wall to the side of the bar. Lucy approached the counter and nodded to the woman on the other side.

"Yes, love?" The barmaid looked to be in her late fifties with flat broad features that looked almost Slavic.

"I booked a room." The woman frowned and leaned forward. Raising her voice so the barmaid could hear her over the racket, Lucy tried again. "I've booked a room. I'm Lucy. Lucy Hush."

"Oh yeah." The woman nodded. "Come into the lounge."

Lucy followed the woman past the bar where two men in hi-vis vests stared blankly at the screen. As she passed, one of the men, a heavy-set guy in his thirties, glanced up.

"How's it going?" He grinned and elbowed the man next to him.

Lucy's first instinct was to ignore him and keep moving, but seeing his work clothes gave her a better idea. She stopped moving and turned so she was standing to his right.

"I'm going very well." She forced a smile that she knew was friendly and interested at the same time.

The guy looked surprised and more than a little pleased. "Yeah?"

"Yeah." Lucy held his gaze, noticing the tiny streaks of red crossing the whites of his eyes. "Do you work around here?"

The man picked up his beer and took a sip before answering. "Yeah, out at the quarry." He spun around on his stool until he was facing her with his knees splayed.

Lucy let go of the suitcase and took a step closer as the man's grin turned into a leer. "I'm looking for someone."

"So's he." His friend, a skinny guy that couldn't have been more than twenty, spoke from the big guy's left.

"Shut-up, Lachie." The man in front of her spoke out of the corner of his mouth while keeping his eyes fixed on Lucy. "Ignore him. What do you need, gorgeous?"

The sharp odour of hops and grass filled the bar, but over the heavy scent of beer, Lucy could smell the man's sweat. She kept the smile fixed in place and continued. "I'm looking for my brother. I just wondered if you've seen him."

The guy leaned back. His sizable belly hung over his navy work pants, straining the buttons on his shirt. "What's his name?"

"Tim Hush." Lucy tried to keep her tone relaxed and friendly, but it was difficult with the constant din of the TV. "He would have been passing through town about four or five days ago." Lucy shrugged. "Maybe looking for work."

The leer evaporated and the big guy clamped his knees together. "Nope. Haven't seen him." He turned back to the race.

Lucy looked over the guy's shoulder at his younger friend, but his eyes were also fixed back on the screen. "I've got a photo here." She reached into her handbag and pulled out a small photograph. "His hair is a bit longer now, but his face is pretty clear. Sometimes he calls himself McMurphy." She held out the image, hoping the big guy would look at it.

"Nope. Haven't seen him." The guy answered with his eyes averted. On the screen, horses were galloping down a muddy looking track.

"You haven't looked at what I'm holding." Lucy didn't know what the guy's problem was. One minute he was overly friendly and the next he wouldn't even look at her. "Here." She held the photo up higher. "Just take a look. Maybe he came to the quarry looking for work or... or here." She waved the photo at the otherwise empty room. "He might have come in for a beer. Just—"

"They told you they haven't seen him." The barmaid who'd been silent up until now spoke from the archway that led out of the bar. "Do you want the room or not?"

"Okay. Yes. Just give me a second." Lucy was starting to get a weird feeling; uncertainty twisted in her gut. Maybe the big guy was pissed off when he realised she wasn't interested in him, but that didn't explain his friend's reaction *or* the barmaid's. It seemed that by mentioning Tim she'd offended them all in some way.

"Look." Lucy could see she wasn't getting anywhere, but it wasn't in her nature to take no for an answer. "Here's my card." She pulled her business card out of her wallet and put it on the bar. "If you remember anything..." The man wouldn't look at her now, so she let her words trail off and waited.

"We haven't seen any drifters." The younger man turned his gaze off the screen and found her eyes. "He told you, now I'm telling you." There was a tone in his voice, almost threatening in the way he nailed each word.

Lucy rolled her shoulders. "Who said he was a drifter?" For a few seconds there was silence, the only sound the clatter of the race caller's voice.

"Angie?" The big guy looked over at the barmaid.

"Okay. That's it." The barmaid, Angie, took hold of Lucy's arm. "Stop bothering my punters."

Lucy thought about pulling her arm away and telling the barmaid to fuck off, but the only other place she'd seen with rooms available was a ramshackle motel. Besides, judging by the two guys' reaction they knew something.

"Okay. Sorry." Lucy gave Angie an apologetic smile and let the woman guide her out of the bar and into the lounge.

Ten minutes later, after some apologising, Lucy tossed her suitcase on the bed and flipped open the lid. The room over the bar was in need of new carpet and a paint job, but spacious and clean. She pulled out her laptop and set it up on the small desk under the room's only window.

At almost six o'clock, darkness blackened the pane. Lucy leaned forward and caught a glimpse of the moon, impossibly large and surrounded by brilliant spots of silver. Tomorrow would be the seventh day since she'd heard from her brother. She forced herself not to dwell on what might have happened to him. Instead, she dragged her gaze back to the computer and began making notes.

As a journalist she was in the habit of writing up a daily log of interviews and research. When she began to transcribe her encounter in the pub, Lucy's finger faltered. The younger man, the one called Lachie, mentioned drifters. Why use that word? She typed the question and highlighted it in yellow. It was something she intended to find out.

By the time she'd finished with her notes it was almost seven p.m. With no time for a shower, Lucy ran a comb through her long brown hair and applied a dab of lip gloss. She still wasn't sure about Damon, but after meeting the locals she was looking forward to a friendly face.

* * *

Damon arrived just on seven. Lucy watched him enter the pub and pause, head up and shoulders squared. He looked confident and at ease with his surroundings. When his eyes landed on her, he nodded and headed her way. On the trip into town she'd been too shaken up to really notice how attractive he was. But now, sitting across from him, Lucy couldn't help studying his whiskey-coloured eyes and the way they seemed to warm under the artificial lights.

Not wanting to be caught staring, she let her gaze float around the room. The two men from earlier were gone, replaced by a few more guys in hi-vis vests, and an assortment of couples and groups. Angie was still behind the bar. Lucy caught the woman looking at her and flashed her a smile. Damon saw the smile and looked over his shoulder.

"Making friends already?"

"Hardly." Lucy grimaced. "The locals are not what I'd call friendly. Not so far." She waved away his questioning look. "Let's get our drinks and order dinner and I'll tell you all about it."

They ordered the special; chicken parmigiana and chips with two pints of beer. When the food arrived, Lucy recounted her conversation with the two men in the pub.

"I have the feeling they know something." She pushed the chips around on her plate, not really feeling hungry. "They were hostile, like they were hiding something."

"Maybe they just don't like drifters." Damon picked up his beer and took a long swallow. "Some of these towns are funny about unemployed people showing up and camping illegally."

"Mm… maybe." Lucy didn't think that was the reason. She'd been a journalist long enough to smell a lead. "What about you? Did you hear anything?"

He shook his head. "No, nothing."

Lucy let out a long breath. "First thing in the morning, I'm going to the police."

When Damon drained the last of his beer, Lucy pushed back her chair and stood. "I need some air." She glanced over at the bar and noticed Angie engaged in conversation with a man with thinning red hair. There was more Lucy had wanted to share with Damon, but didn't think the pub was the place to do it. "Do you feel like taking a walk?"

Damon nodded and waited while she shrugged into her dark green puffer coat. As they left the bar, Lucy noticed Angie and the red-headed man watching them.

The night air was a cold slap that made her zip up her jacket and stuff her hands in her pockets. They walked along the street side by side, almost touching but not quite as a smattering of cars and utes drove by. For a few minutes neither of them spoke.

"What's so special about your birthday?" The question took her by surprise. He seemed to know just when to spring an enquiry. If she didn't know better, she'd think Damon had a reporter's instincts.

Lucy shrugged. "Family stuff." It wasn't exactly a lie, more of an understatement. But right now, with Tim missing, she couldn't afford to let herself sink back into painful memories.

Without heading in any particular direction, they turned the corner and entered a grassy area with a few benches. It looked like some sort of park, but with only a single light beaming down from a recycled tree-pole it was impossible to see what the shadows hid.

Lucy made a bee-line for the benches and sat. It occurred to her that she was taking a risk wandering off into the night with a man she barely knew. But if he wanted to hurt her, he'd had plenty of opportunities on the drive into town. Besides, her instincts told her Damon was safe. And one thing she'd learned to do was trust her instincts.

"So..." Lucy patted the wooden bench slats for him to sit. "Tell me about yourself."

Damon chuckled, a deep throaty sound that reminded her of an old jazz singer. He sat beside her, closer than she'd expected.

"Well." He clasped his hands between his legs, leaning forward. "What do you want to know?"

"How come you're wandering the roads with a bunch of French backpackers? Don't get me wrong. I'm not judging your lifestyle. I just can't quite work you out."

"I'm not that complicated. I left the Armed Forces six years ago and since then I work for myself."

She watched his profile as he spoke, noticing how still he managed to remain.

"I have a good pension and some savings, so I guess I'm lucky enough to be able to just do my own thing." He turned his head and gave her a lopsided smile. "What about you?"

She couldn't help being impressed by his deftness. He'd managed to answer the question without giving much away, then quickly turned the conversation back on her.

"I'm a journalist." Lucy dumped her handbag on her lap and pulled out the cigarette packet. "I work for Channel 12 as a crime reporter." She turned the packet over in her hand but didn't open it. "Sort of behind the scenes research, writing, that sort of thing." She glanced at Damon, watching his profile again.

"So, what does your training tell you about Night Town?" He sat back and turned to look at her. The yellowy streetlight set his face in shadows.

"I don't know about my training." She stuffed the cigarette pack back in her bag. "But my gut tells me whatever happened to Tim took place here." She pointed a finger down at the ground to indicate the town.

"So tomorrow you talk to the cops."

Lucy stood. "Yeah. Then I'll do a bit of digging – see if I can find out more about this place." The temperature had taken a dip. The night air made her lips numb. "What about you? What are your plans, Damon?"

He stood and pushed a strand of hair off her forehead. His touch made her want to shiver, but she managed to suppress the urge. "I'll hang around for a few days." His hand slid downwards and grasped hers. "Come on. I'll walk you back."

Chapter Four

Lucy was up, showered and dressed by eight a.m. When Damon walked her back to the Royal the night before, she'd given him her business card, half expecting him to make a pass at her, but instead he said goodnight and left her at the pub door. It wasn't until she climbed the stairs and entered her room that she realised she hadn't told him she was staying at the pub.

Now, as cool morning light flooded her room, it occurred to her that when she told Damon about her encounter with the two guys and the barmaid, he must have worked out she was staying in the Royal Hotel. No big mystery, but still a little unsettling. She shrugged off the feeling, then slipped her laptop case over her shoulder before heading downstairs. Damon was a distraction, a pleasant one but not what she needed if she was going to focus her mind on finding Tim.

"Morning." Angie caught her as she reached the side door that led to the parking lot.

"Morning, Angie." Lucy gave the woman a tight smile and kept moving.

"So, you're a reporter." The woman's words stopped Lucy at the door. "I thought you were here looking for your brother?"

Lucy let her hand rest on the door handle, but turned her head. "I am looking for my brother and, yes, I'm a reporter." The woman's attitude was really starting to wear on her. "Is that a problem?"

Angie pursed her lips, pulling the skin taunt over her flat features. "Not for me."

Lucy thought about asking the woman what she meant, but decided she'd wasted enough time on the barmaid. "Good." She pushed the door open and left without looking back.

Using the Saab's navigation system, Lucy managed to find the police station in less than five minutes. Set back one street from the town centre, the small white-washed building sat next to a more modern-looking library. Lucy parked on the street and entered the station to the sound of a ringing telephone and the slam of a door somewhere in the rear of the building.

Like most stations in Western Australia, this one had a front counter that was reminiscent of an old post office. The air was heavy with the smell of coffee and what might have been toner. Lucy took a few seconds to scan the area before stepping up to the counter. A uniformed officer looked up from his desk and greeted her with a blank stare. There was one other desk in the small station that sat unoccupied and stacked with files. A narrow corridor draped in shadows led to the back of the building.

"Hi." Lucy waited, but the officer didn't respond. *This is crazy.* "I'd like to report someone missing." She returned his blank stare and waited.

The officer stood and made a show of hitching his pants before ambling towards the counter. He looked familiar, but she couldn't quite place him.

"Name?" He reached under the counter and produced a slab of note paper and a pen.

"My name is Lucy. Lucy Hush. My br—"

He held up his hand and she noticed the man's palms were nearly as wide and flat as a dinner plate. At the top of the page he wrote her name. "Okay. Who's missing?" His tone was disinterested, impatient. Lucy couldn't help wondering if she was wasting her time.

"My brother. Tim... Timothy Hush. He's been missing for seven days." She waited while he wrote on the pad. She slipped the laptop off her shoulder and set it down on the counter. "I have a photo that might help." She started unzipping the case.

"Just hold your horses." His tone was gruff now, almost warning. "If you want help, you'd better slow down and let me do my job."

Lucy shook her head, trying to make sense of what the man was saying. His truculent attitude was off-putting to say the least. She was used to dealing with the police *and*, as a reporter, being given the cold shoulder, but this was different. She hadn't identified herself as being with the press. There was no reason she could see for the officer's hostility.

"What's your name, officer?" She kept her voice calm, knowing it would do no good to escalate the situation, but unable to tolerate the man's rudeness any longer.

He tossed the pen on the pad and put his hands on the counter palms down. In that moment Lucy recognised him as the man she'd seen talking to Angie in the pub last night. No doubt the barmaid had filled him in on her occupation.

"My name is Senior Constable Gordon Holsey." He held her gaze. His pale eyes reminded her of a piece of broken glass, almost colourless.

"Senior Constable Holsey." She spoke slowly, keeping the anger out of her voice, but unable to stop it rising. "Would you mind telling me why you're being so officious?"

Holsey's reddish skin flushed, turning almost crimson, and his lips quivered. "I'll tell you something for your own good." He leaned forward and she could smell cheese on his breath. "You'd b—"

A door at the rear of the station thumped open and another officer appeared in the narrow hallway. Holsey glanced over his shoulder and let his hands drop from the counter. Lucy had the distinct impression she'd just escaped a rather nasty tirade.

The other officer, tall and muscular with closely cut dark hair, approached the counter. "Thanks, Holsey. I'll take over." He held an air of authority and spoke with the confidence of one used to being obeyed.

"It's okay, boss. I was just telling this... *lady*." Holsey stumbled over the last word.

"No." The other officer, a good five years younger than Holsey, cut him off. "I'd like you to finish that report and get it on my desk within the hour."

Not waiting for a response, the officer giving the orders turned his attention to Lucy. "I'm Senior Sergeant Day." He stepped around the counter. "Please, come into my office."

Lucy nodded. "Thank you." She picked up her laptop case and snatched a glimpse at Holsey. His eyes were on something on the far wall, fixed and unmoving. She noticed a vein in his neck, thick and purple, crawling its way up his throat.

Senior Sergeant Day led Lucy to the rear of the station and into his office. He closed the door behind them. She had the feeling she'd just witnessed a glimpse of an ongoing power struggle.

"Please, have a seat." He motioned to the seat in front of his desk.

Lucy took her time, unzipping her coat and settling into the chair. She stretched out the moment, giving herself time to glance around and take in all of Day's office. She noticed that the pin board on the far wall held only two items. A calendar to the left of the desk was the generic type usually given away free at pharmacies. If anything, Day's office looked sparse.

"Now." He clasped his hands together and placed them on top of the desk. "Did you want to file a report?" His eyes were dark, almost the colour of coal. The contrast made the whites look startling.

"Yes." Lucy set her laptop case on his desk. "It's my brother. I'd like to report him missing." She glanced at Day's mug half-filled with what appeared to be white coffee. The cup was as plain and as generic as the calendar.

"Okay." He turned to the computer on his left and tapped the keyboard. "I'll need some details. Yours first. Start with full name and address."

Lucy reeled off her details, noticing there were no personal photos in the office. The sparseness of the room and the exchange with Holsey indicated that Senior Sergeant Day was new, not only new to the position, but also probably new in town. She hoped it meant he'd be more accommodating than the locals.

Day stopped typing and returned his hands to their former position. "You live in Perth. Did you report your brother's disappearance at your local police station?"

Lucy took a breath and sat back in the chair. She knew this question was coming and was prepared to side-step it. "My brother disappeared in Night Town, so I thought it best to come here." It was half-true. She *had* tried to report Tim as a missing person in Perth, but as soon as she revealed her brother's nomadic lifestyle, the local authorities showed little interest. In fact, the senior officer at her local police station had suggested she go home and wait another week before filing a report. It was then she decided to drive to Night Town and, if necessary, begin the search on her own.

Day nodded, but his face gave nothing away. "Tell me about the disappearance?"

There wasn't much to tell. The details were simple. Tim didn't show up on her birthday on the 20th of June. The last she'd heard from him he'd been in Night Town and ready to head home. Then nothing.

"He's never missed a birthday." She pushed a strand of hair behind her ear. "He wouldn't miss one... Not by choice." A tug of emotion like a hand squeezing her throat caught her off guard and, suddenly, she found herself close to tears. "Something's wrong. It's been seven days." She spread her hands in exasperation. "And nothing."

Day waited before speaking, suggesting he was letting her words sink in. "So, your brother told you he was in Night Town." He paused and Lucy nodded. "You believe something happened to him before he left?"

"It's the only thing that makes sense. Tim always carries ID. If he'd had an accident, been hit by a car or something, they'd have contacted me." She was rushing to get the words out now, desperate to make Day understand. "Once he got to Bunbury or Mandurah, he'd have let me know. But this..." She tapped her finger on Day's desk. "This was the last place he was before all contact stopped."

Before he could answer, Lucy unzipped her laptop case and slid the computer out. "Look at this." She brought up a photograph and spun the screen around so the Senior Sergeant could see. "Tim sent this to me just before he disappeared. I didn't notice the background when I looked at it on my phone, but when I pulled it up on my laptop, look." She tapped the screen.

The photo was a selfie, Tim smiling into the lens, and behind him the strange, key-shaped black sculpture that sat at Night Town's centre.

"You see." Lucy stared at Day, hoping for some sign that he understood.

"This photo proves your brother was here, but not that he never left." Day must have caught the look on her face because he held up a hand. "I'm not saying that you're wrong, just that the photo only proves he was here." He leaned forward, seeming to study the photo. "It's a good place to start, though." He looked up. "I'll need you to email me that."

Lucy clamped her lips together and nodded, knowing if she spoke the tears would come. Day was taking Tim's disappearance seriously. After all the phone calls, the driving, not to mention the angry locals, someone was finally listening. She had the urge to put her head on the desk and weep.

"I'll need some background on your brother. Address, work, friends, that sort of thing." And with that Lucy felt her relief fizzling out like a melted birthday candle.

"My brother..." She didn't know quite how to explain Tim. Not in a way that would make any sense to someone like Day. *No*, she corrected herself. The Senior Sergeant had been fair with her so far. She couldn't write him off yet. "He lives an alternative lifestyle." She saw Day's brows draw together and tried to rush to explain. "He doesn't break any laws." *Except smoking weed.* "He's not crazy *or* stupid. In fact, he has an exceptionally high IQ and an uncanny memory. He... he knows how things work. He's easy-going, but his brain works faster than anyone I've ever met." Lucy let out a breath and forced herself to slow down. "He likes being outdoors." She shrugged. "A hundred years ago he'd have been called a swagman." She forced a laugh, but noticed Day continued to frown.

"I see." He leaned forward and Lucy spotted a scar running up the outside of his left bicep, a jagged angry white line that looked like it had been inflicted with something razor sharp. "So, your brother's a drifter. Is that what you're trying to tell me?"

Lucy thought of at least five kinder ways to describe Tim, but it always came back to that word. "Yes."

"All right. I'll need to know how long he was in town before you think he disappeared."

Lucy was lost for words. "You mean you're... So, you'll look into it?"

He nodded. "You believe your brother is missing *and*," he drew the word out, "it's out of character for him to go this long without contacting you, so there are certainly reasons for me to take this seriously."

"Yes. Okay, good." She smiled. Probably the first real smile she'd managed in the seven days since she received the photo. "What now?"

Day opened a drawer on the right-hand side of the desk. "Here's my card. You can email me the photo at this address." He pushed the card across the desk. "Anything else you think of that might help, including bank account details." He tapped the card. "Put all the information in the email."

Lucy picked up the card and slipped it in the front pocket of her black jeans. "I'll get it to you within the hour."

"All right." Day stood, which Lucy took as an indication the meeting was over. She picked up her laptop and followed him to the door.

"I'll be in touch, most likely by tomorrow afternoon." He paused, his hand resting on the door handle. "I know you're worried, but please leave this to me. Trust me when I say the locals are more likely to respond to my questions than yours."

Standing within a half metre of him, Lucy picked up the scent of something sharp and clean, maybe shaving soap. He was waiting for her to respond, his dark eyes trained on her face. "Okay." She gave him a tight smile.

He hesitated, seeming to want to say something else, but instead opened the door. "I'll walk you out."

* * *

Holsey watched Day walk the woman out of the station. As they passed, he dipped his head and focused on the computer screen. He supposed she was pretty, if you

30

liked pushy women that thought the world belonged to them because their ass was gym-membership tight and they paid a hundred dollars for a haircut.

"Thank you, Senior Sergeant." The woman's voice almost rattled with fake gratitude *and*, by the look on Day's face, the guy was falling for it.

"I'll be in touch." Day held the door and watched the woman leave. Holsey noticed his boss's face in profile. With the early morning light shining through the door, the outline was sharp. Not for the first time Holsey was surprised by how swiftly his boss's expressions could change.

When Day walked back around the counter, Holsey was careful to keep his eyes on the screen.

"I'm going out." Day spoke without stopping, brushing past Holsey's desk and heading for the back door. "Get that report on my desk by nine."

"Where you going?" He knew he shouldn't ask, but Day looked like he was in a hurry and Holsey couldn't resist.

"Mind your own fucking business." The new Senior Sergeant didn't bother turning around.

Holsey listened for the slam of the back door. "Fuck you, too." He pushed back his chair and ambled towards his boss's office.

The lights were off. An eerie blue light lit the windowless room. Drawn by the glow of the computer screen, Holsey approached the desk and sat, making himself comfortable. He tapped the tracker.

"Damn." The computer was password protected. He wasn't really surprised. Still, it would have been nice to have a nose around.

Rather than hurrying back to typing out the report, he leaned back and put his feet up on the Senior Sergeant's desk. Day was a real mystery package and Holsey didn't like mysteries. Something wasn't right with the new boss;

he could almost smell it. Like the guy's faggy shaving soap
— the smell set Holsey's teeth on edge.

Chapter Five

Lucy wanted coffee – hot, milky and sweet – but she had more pressing matters to deal with. After leaving the police station, she ducked next door and paid a visit to the library.

A lone librarian, a painfully thin woman in a trim blue blouse and navy cardigan, sat behind a wood veneer counter, typing with her gaze bouncing between a stack of books and the screen. As Lucy approached, the woman looked up and gave her a curt smile. The slim gold badge on the librarian's blouse identified her as Ruth.

"Good morning." The librarian's tone was pleasant, but the agreeable note didn't quite reach the woman's eyes.

"Hi." Lucy gave what she hoped was a charming smile. "Can I set up my laptop? I need to use your Wi-Fi."

The librarian's eyes skimmed over Lucy's face and outfit with practiced speed. As if satisfied with what she saw, the woman's demeanour softened. "Yes. Of course." She picked up a card and handed it to Lucy. "Here's the code. There should be space available in the daily section."

As she leaned forward and pointed to the rear of the one-level building, Lucy caught a whiff of tobacco. The smell set off a wave of craving that almost made her gasp.

"Thank you." Lucy hefted the laptop case and turned away.

She set herself up at a small cubby-hole-type desk near a rack of newspapers and international magazines. The only other occupant of the daily section was an elderly man with a newspaper spread on his lap and a pair of bifocals dangerously close to tipping off the end of his nose.

Satisfied that she had privacy, Lucy logged on and accessed the Internet. She began by firing off an email to Senior Sergeant Day, outlining as much of Tim's history as she thought safe. Then, after attaching the photo, she pressed send.

With the email out of the way, she turned her attention on research. Within a minute or so she found a brief history of the town under a story about the logging industry. The article offered little in terms of information other than that the town was founded in 1872 by a man named William Nightmesser and the current population, which was around four thousand. Lucy scratched her chin. The name was familiar, but she couldn't quite place it.

Pushing on, she found a few photos of the town. Most included the strange sculpture from Tim's selfie. One of the images was a shot of the supermarket she'd seen on the main street. Below the shop's name, *Freshco*, were the words *Nightmesser Holdings*. Lucy leaned back in her seat and crossed her arms.

So, after close to two hundred years, Nightmesser was still a name with some clout in the small town. Lucy decided to search the name. It might be a dead end, but she really had nothing close to a lead. After a brief search she found a number of articles. One dated 2014 reported the dedication of a new addition to the town hall and the other, a charitable event sponsored by Nightmesser Holdings to raise money for a local girl in need of a heart and lung transplant. Another story dated 2013 detailed Nightmesser's sponsorship of a new chapel to be used for ecumenical services for the people of Night Town. There were several more articles, all concerning donations to the town by Samson Nightmesser.

As she scrolled through the stories, Lucy found another older article dated October 1989, this one detailing the death of Nathan Nightmesser aged eighty-six. There was a photo, a black and white image of a stern-looking elderly man standing next to a vintage Holden. To his right stood a boy of about twelve, wearing a school uniform. The frail-looking boy was looking to the side where a woman in some sort of uniform stood with her arms folded around her body. The article went on to say the photo was taken ten years earlier when Nathan Nightmesser opened the limestone quarry on the outskirts of town. Lucy frowned, wondering why they used such an old photo. Nathan, it said, passed peacefully at home and was survived by his son, Samson.

Lucy copied the article and photo and pasted it to her desktop. Based on what she'd read, it seemed Nathan Nightmesser died almost thirty years ago, leaving his estate to his son. Since then Samson had been a generous benefactor, donating regularly to the town's infrastructure, as well as providing jobs at the quarry. Lucy pinched the bridge of her nose. While the town's history was mildly interesting, she doubted it would help her find her brother.

Time, she decided, for a coffee. After making a few notes on her progress, she packed up her laptop and headed out of the library. On her way past the desk, she noticed the librarian had left her post and was in the office on the telephone. Clearly visible through the glass wall, the woman seemed to be in the midst of a heated conversation.

Lucy hesitated, watching the woman shaking her head, her short red hair unmoving as she jabbed her finger in the air. The librarian looked up and saw Lucy watching her. The woman's mouth fell open and she turned her back and bent her head as though whispering. *Either I'm losing it or this town is full of drama.*

Lucy hurried out of the library and turned left, noticing a brass plaque on the face-brick wall. *Dedicated by Samson Nightmesser, 2006.* For some reason the recurring name made her nervous and set off a sinking feeling like she was caught in an old horror movie where aliens take over the world by slipping pods under their beds while people slept. It was a ridiculous thought, one she tried to laugh off while at the same time hastening her pace as she crossed the parking lot.

Not really sure where to go for a decent cup of coffee, she drove back to the town centre. On the way, the scene in the library played over in her mind. Something in the way the woman's mouth dropped open when she saw Lucy watching made Lucy think the librarian was talking about her.

She turned onto the main street and drove past the Royal Hotel. The idea of going back to her room was less than appealing. Besides, her stomach was howling for food and her nerves jangling for a cigarette. Ignoring the nicotine craving, she pulled up a few car lengths away from a small café. The name on the faded red awning said Hodge Podge. *At least it's not called Nightmesser Coffee.* She let out a nervous laugh and climbed out of the car.

Inside, the café was warm and decorated in an eclectic mix of shabby chic and abstract paintings. Lucy ordered a coffee, and a bacon sandwich, which she devoured at a table near the window. As she sipped her coffee she watched an endless run of traffic fill the main street while the sun ducked in and out of a cloudy sky. In the time she'd been sitting at the table she clocked three trucks bearing the name Nightmesser. If she wasn't in town to find her brother, she'd probably be able to put together a story on one family's monopoly on a small town.

What, she wondered, had Tim made of this place? And why of all the small towns in the south-west had he decided to stop here and take a selfie? Even as a child he'd been fascinated by how things worked, especially clocks and locks. Maybe that key-like sculpture drew him to the town. She touched her fingertips to her temples, trying to massage out something tangible, a reason for Tim's visit to Night Town. Her brother was a nomad, but he usually had reasons for his decisions. She remembered him telling her that he'd camped on the outskirts of Cowaramup, spending almost two months drifting in and out of the settlement and the huge expanse of bushland surrounding the small village.

Lucy pulled out her phone and opened the photo he'd sent her last year. Tim smiling into the lens, his arm draped around one of the village's forty-two life-size fiberglass Friesian cows. *Anywhere crazy enough to have so many huge cows on their main street makes me feel more normal.* She could almost hear her brother's voice, that soft, laid-back tone she knew so well. And just like that the tears were flowing, running down her cheeks and dripping off her chin in big wet plops.

She lowered her head and dug through her coat pocket, searching for a tissue, hand shaking as the emotion overtook her. Around her, other customers continued to chat and laugh. Their voices, a chorus of happiness, only heightened her despair. For the first time in seven days she let herself think about the reality of never seeing Tim again.

If she'd been alone in her room, Lucy would have put her head in her hands and wept, but in full view of a shop full of strangers, she struggled to keep herself in check. Usually able to control her feelings in even the most harrowing situations, she now found herself rushing from the café, head down and shoulders trembling.

Once in the car she pulled up the hood on her puffer coat and let the tears fall. She'd worked so long and hard to keep things going, to keep her and Tim together. Even when it seemed he was falling apart, Lucy had managed to be the brave one. Since the age of twenty-one she played the role of mother more than sister. But sitting in her car alone and desperate, she realised she was just as fractured as Tim. Only he'd let his feelings surface, dropping out of school, and giving up on a normal life while she'd pushed her emotions down by striving to get a job and work her way up the ranks.

Her life, she realised, was just as messed up as Tim's. No, she corrected herself. Her life was *more* messed up than her brother's because at least Tim had found a way to be content. He was brave enough to live by his own rules.

Her soulful little brother, always kind-hearted, but never at rest in the hustle and bustle of the city. Lucy's heart lurched and, for a moment, she couldn't breathe. If he was gone she'd be alone in the world. The prospect was almost more than she could bear. She gulped in a breath. *No, he's not gone.*

"He's not gone." She said the words aloud. "He's not gone." The second time her voice was stronger.

As her breathing evened out, her phone shrilled, the sound startling in the confines of the car. Sniffing back tears, she fumbled out the mobile only to hesitate before answering. Frowning at the unknown number, she accepted the call.

"Hi, Lucy." The voice was immediately familiar.

"Damon, hi." She tried to keep her tone steady, desperately hoping he wouldn't hear the snuffle of tears.

But Damon wasn't to be fooled. "What's happened? Is it Tim?"

"No. No. I'm… just having a moment." She tried for a laugh, but it came out wet and pathetic. "There's no news on Tim. I got a bit overwhelmed is all."

"Where are you? I'll come and meet you." The concern in his voice set off a fresh stream of tears.

She considered telling him no and insisting she was fine, but isn't that what she'd always done? Pretend she was fine and stuff down the emotions? Maybe if she'd let someone help her when tragedy struck her family, things would be different now and her brother might be thinking about getting married and settling down instead of... She couldn't finish the thought, not if she wanted to hold her composure.

"I'm sitting in my car near a café on the main street. It's called Hodge Podge. The café, not my car." It was a silly joke, but to her relief Damon chuckled.

"I'll be there in less than ten minutes. Wait for me."

Damon arrived in six minutes, tapping on the fogged-up driver's window then dashing around to the passenger side. Lucy took a long breath and pulled back her hood.

"Jesus, it's freezing out there." Damon folded himself into the car and slammed the door. Turning to look at her, his expression was a mixture of concern and something else, maybe surprise.

To her relief he sat in silence, his presence comforting without bombarding her with words. After a moment he placed his hand on the console, palm up. Lucy let her hand hover above his, their skin only centimetres apart. She trailed her finger along the lines in Damon's palm before placing her hand in his.

His skin was warm, his palm rough as if it'd known manual work. Damon closed his fingers around hers and they continued to sit in silence. Lucy closed her eyes and let her mind rest and her body enjoy the sensation of being connected to someone other than Tim.

A horn blared on the street and Lucy's eyes flew open.

"Do you want to take a drive?" Damon asked, still holding her hand.

* * *

For the second time in two days Lucy allowed Damon to drive her car. This, she imagined, is what it's like to be married, sharing the driving chore. It was a silly school-girl thought that took her by surprise.

"Where are we going?" She watched the town disappear and the road narrow then sink into the wildness of the forest.

Damon took a second before answering. "I want to show you something and then we need to talk." His gaze was on the road, making it impossible for her to see his eyes.

"That sounds serious." Only minutes ago, she'd felt connected to the man in a way she wouldn't have thought possible, but now something had shifted and she felt a quiver of uncertainty. "What's this all about?"

"It's not much further. It's easier if I show you."

They were less than ten minutes out of town when the road diverged. Straight ahead lay a heavily used limestone track, to the right a narrow bituminised road that bore no name and had the look of a private entry. Damon slowed and turned right, nosing the Saab onto the narrow pea gravel shoulder.

As he cut the engine and turned towards her, Lucy flinched and her hand grabbed for the door handle. The confused look on Damon's face turned into amusement.

"Jesus, Lucy. I didn't bring you out here to attack you." There was humour tinged with a note of surprise.

"Okay." She let herself relax, feeling rather silly for flinching like a skittish teenager. *At least I'm over the floods of tears.* "What *are* we doing here?"

He jerked his thumb over his left shoulder. "That way leads to the quarry." He nodded at the entry road. "And this way to Nightmesser House. Behind the quarry and private residence is forty acres of forest all owned by Samson Nightmesser."

"Wait a minute." Lucy shook her head, trying to make sense of what he was telling her. "How do you know all this?"

"That," he said, turning the engine on, "is what I want to talk to you about. But not here."

He executed a three-point turn and they were back on the road to town, but rather than entering Night Town, Damon turned left onto a dirt track and stopped the car.

The emotion that overwhelmed her in the café had abated, not completely, but enough for Lucy to begin thinking more clearly. Damon was driving the roads with a certainty that came from experience. He knew where the quarry was *and* how to reach Samson Nightmesser's house. It was clear that he was no drifter.

Lucy didn't like being lied to or manipulated. With her nerves still raw with worry she felt a spark of anger that threatened to burn out of control.

"Look." She turned in her seat and put one hand on the dashboard. "I've had enough of this. Tell me what's going on or get out of my car, because my patience is really starting to wear thin."

"I'm sorry." Damon held her gaze. "I haven't been honest with you..."

"I'm starting to see that." Lucy wasn't sure she liked where this was heading. Ever since the day before when he appeared at her car window something about their meeting had bugged her.

"I was telling the truth about the French backpackers. I left my car at a mate's house in Busselton and hitched a ride. They really did abandon me in the bush." Damon rubbed his chin, the bristles rasping under his fingers. "I was in Night Town the day before we met. I should have told you, but the coincidence of meeting you and discovering we were both here for the same reason..." He let his eyes drift to the front window, appearing to be watching something on the dirt track. "...it threw me and I wasn't sure."

"What do you mean the same reason?" She kept her stare pinned on his face. "I'm here looking for my brother.

Are you saying you're looking for Tim? Because that makes no sense."

"No. Not Tim." Damon reached inside his jacket and produced a photograph. "I'm looking for a man named Aidan." He held the picture out for her to take.

Lucy took hold of the image, still not sure she believed or understood anything Damon was saying. When her eyes fell on the photo she let out a gasp, a small sound, one of shock and pain. The man in the picture was similar enough to her brother to make Lucy's heart jump. He had the same shaggy hair, a worn beanie pulled down around his ears. He was so like Tim, she felt a fresh crop of tears sting her eyes.

"He disappeared six months ago. His mother received a call from him shortly before he vanished."

She was only half listening to him now, intent on the image. Looking closer, she could see the similarities were only superficial. The man in the photo was older than Tim, heavier around the chin, and his eyes were dark and troubled.

"He, Aidan, mentioned Night Town."

Lucy's head snapped up. "He disappeared here?" She still held the photo, the image cold in her hand. "In Night Town, just like my…" The air inside the Saab was warm. Lucy's throat tightened and suddenly breathing was a chore. She let the photo drop onto the console and opened the car door.

Stumbling out onto the track, a burst of wind caught her hair and whipped it around her face. The photo, another missing man, confirmed her darkest fears. Tim wasn't just missing. He wasn't merely injured or lost, he'd been abducted. Her mind threw up images: shallow graves and pale-faced families weeping through television interviews. She'd seen so much of it in her career. Now it was her family. Her *only* family.

"Lucy." Damon's voice beside her was a whisper of compassion. She turned to face him, seeing her fears reflected in his eyes. "It doesn't mean Tim's dead. He's only been missing seven days."

She tried to focus on what Damon was saying, but the words were hollow, caught on the wind and meaningless. The bush and trees surrounding the track were like an endless wall, and somewhere amongst the wild tangle... A shiver started in her legs, spreading upwards until her body was vibrating.

Damon was still talking. "There's a chance we can find him. He may still be alive."

She caught the word chance and held it. Nodding now, she wrapped her arms around her body. It *had* only been seven days, maybe less. The possibility of finding Tim was still real.

Damon touched her arm and she jumped. "Sorry."

Lucy rolled her shoulders. "What else do you know?"

They sat in the car and talked for what seemed like hours while outside a soft smattering of rain began to fall. The regular patter of drops mingled with Damon's voice, not softening his words, but adding to their impact.

"After Aidan's mother contacted me, I did some research. I've come up with a list of men who may have been close to Night Town before they went missing." He took a long breath before continuing. "I found three cases over the last six years and..." He tapped Aidan's photo. "They were all drifters, disaffected men whose families were unable to pinpoint the exact date they went missing. All disappeared in this part of the south-west."

"Wait a minute." The part of her that worked on facts and patterns kicked back in. "How can there be that many missing men, all a similar type, yet as a member of the press I've never heard about the case?"

Damon's voice changed. There was a note of anger in his words. "There is no case. The south-west is a huge region and these men were easy targets. With their background, mental illness and drug use, their disappearances were never taken seriously enough for anyone to look closely."

Lucy thought of the way the cop at her local station had treated her when she tried to report Tim as a missing person. It was easy to imagine men like her brother slipping through the cracks. An image began to form in her mind. A sinister figure targeting and preying on troubled men, pouncing on them in their weakness and using society's complacency as a shield against exposure.

Even as the thoughts formed, her brain was already putting a story together. "We need to get this story in front of my editor. If we can get a spotlight on what's going on here, the police will have to take it seriously." There was still hope. She could feel the energy flooding her body, a familiar rush that came with the high of breaking a big story. Only this time it wasn't just a story. Her brother's life was on the line. "I'll need to see your research and call my editor."

"Wait." Damon caught her hand as she reached for her handbag. "This is all just loose facts. We can't prove anything until we have more information." His grasp was firm on her arm. "If we move too quickly and there's nothing to back up what we're proposing, we'll blow any chance of getting the cops on board." He let go of her and shrugged. "Or worse, this guy, the one who's got your brother, if he gets a whiff of police attention…" He trailed off without finishing the thought.

"He'll get rid of Tim and disappear?" She finished the thought for him.

Damon didn't answer. He didn't have to. They both knew he was right and all they had was a few missing men with nothing to link them. Something that had been on her mind earlier flitted across the edge of her thoughts. If she hadn't been so overwhelmed with emotion back at the café, she might have latched onto it sooner.

She fastened her seatbelt. "I still need to see your research."

Chapter Six

The motel room was as she'd imagined: aging and worn. The double bed, unmade and in disarray, was flanked by a cheap desk on one side and a nightstand on the other. Damon moved over to the window and jerked the curtains wide, letting the early afternoon light chase away the shadows.

"Okay." Damon was straight to business, stripping off his jacket and tossing it on the bed. "This is what I've put together so far." He pulled a blue folder out of his leather pack and set it on the desk. "I've got soft copies of everything on a flash drive, but this..." He tapped the folder. "This will help you get a picture of what I've found."

Lucy watched Damon move around the room. He seemed bigger when contained in the small space. There was still so much she didn't know about him and how he happened to be in the right place at the right time. She glanced at the folder, eager to search its contents for anything that might lead her to Tim. But before she could trust Damon's research, she had to know more about the man.

Still standing near the door, Lucy unzipped her coat. "Look, before this goes any further I need answers." Trusting people didn't come naturally to her and, as much as – like a woman dangling from a crumbling ledge – she wanted to grasp hold of Damon's help, her instincts told her to take care.

Damon sat on the bed and spread his arms wide. "Fire away." The light fell on his face, revealing tiny lines around his eyes. In spite of the situation, she wondered what those lines would feel like under her fingers.

Momentarily off balance, Lucy was at a loss for words. She covered her discomfort by removing her coat and draping it over her arm. "Well, you can start by telling me what you were really doing on the road yesterday, and then the missing guy... Uh..."

"Aidan." He filled in the name.

"Yes, Aidan. Why are you looking for him?" She glanced over at the file as if the promised information might evaporate before she had the chance to read it. "You said you were ex-military working for yourself. So, what's your connection to this guy?"

He turned to the window, his eyes on the winter sky. "Aidan Morris is his name. He served under me in the army. I haven't seen him in years. I barely recognised him in the photo. When he was discharged, I lost contact. That's on me." He turned away from the window. "Lucy, I wish you'd sit down."

The change in direction took her by surprise. She threw her coat on the bed and turned the chair in front of the desk around so it was facing him. "Better?" she asked, sitting with her back to the window.

He nodded. "Aidan had a rough time. He saw things that messed him up. Did things." Damon scratched the back of his neck. "We all did things that followed us, but with him it was different." He hesitated for an instant. His voice almost cracked on the last words. "It changed him."

Lucy found herself nodding. She'd never been in a war zone, but she'd seen things that couldn't be wiped away. As Damon talked about the things that drove Aidan out of the army and into a life of wandering, she couldn't help seeing the similarities between the man Damon was looking for and her brother. Both men living a half-life on the edge of society because the past filled too much of their lives.

"I got a call from Aidan's mother about two weeks ago," Damon continued. "She said she found my number in some of his things. She was desperate, didn't know who else to ask." He jerked his chin in Lucy's direction. "Like you, she couldn't get the police to do much outside taking her son's details and telling her to wait." His voice was low, almost a whisper. So different from his usual casual tone. "I agreed to help, do what I could. In another life, finding people that didn't want to be found was what I did." He leaned back on his elbows. "So that's why I'm here. And, I was telling the truth about the French backpackers. They did abandon me out there." He gave her a crooked smile and his face changed from intense to mischievous. "I skipped the part about using them as a way of backtracking into Night Town as a drifter."

By the time Damon finished, long shadows were creeping across the small desk and the folder he'd placed there. If Lucy had any doubts about the man's honesty, the way he described the young man he'd known in the army drove them away. What remained was a feeling of connection to the man on the bed. A connection because they were seeking the same thing: a lonely soul forgotten by the rest of the world.

"So how do you explain our meeting on the road?" She held up a finger. "Be careful because I don't believe in coincidences." It was true. She had never fallen in with the popular belief that things happen for a reason and that there was some cosmic force guiding people's lives. Yet, now in light of what Damon had revealed, part of her wanted to believe they'd found each other for a reason. And maybe that reason was to bring her brother home alive.

"I can't explain it." He leaned forward and let his hands dangle between his knees. "I don't believe in coincidences either, but..." He drew out the word. "I've seen enough weird stuff in my life to know when to grab something that feels right. This feels right and that's good enough for me."

Before Lucy could respond, he was on his feet. "You read the file. I'm going to get us something to eat and drink." He pulled on his jacket and headed for the door.

"Whiskey," Lucy called as he opened the door. Damon stopped and gave her a questioning look. "Scottish, please."

Once alone, Lucy turned on the lights, pulled the curtains, and took a notepad and pen out of her handbag. She sat at the desk, opened the file and flicked through the pages, noticing print-outs of several news articles containing photographs, as well as a map, a list of names, some with phone numbers and a few pages of handwritten notes. It wasn't much, but more than she'd had a few hours ago.

She began by reading the articles and taking a few notes. The first was a short piece from the Daily Post in Busselton, detailing the disappearance of a man named Thomas Whelldon. According to the article, Whelldon, aged twenty-two, was last seen leaving a pub in Busselton in the early hours one night in May 2012. The article gave some background on the man, including his history of drug use and bipolar disorder. Rather than focusing on his disappearance, the reporter noted that Thomas Whelldon was a homeless man with a penchant for wandering the south-west, supporting his drug habit by begging. The article included a blurry photo of Whelldon in profile, most likely cropped from a larger image.

Lucy let out a tired breath and picked up the next article. This one, from a small local paper in Margaret River, was similar to the last only a few paragraphs longer. Tyson Jacobs, age thirty-six, was last seen in Gracetown in 2014. As Lucy read the scant details, a whisper of dread – cold and tight – curled itself around her heart. Jacobs was involved in a car accident in 2001, leaving him with head injuries and short-term memory problems. Problems that prevented him from holding down a regular job. The accompanying photo, a clear shot of Jacobs, showed a man that looked frail and much older than his thirty-six years, facing the camera holding a stubby in one hand and a cigarette in the other.

Lucy scribbled a few notes and moved on to the next article. This one, the most recent, dated the 12th of February 2016 had the headline: *Son Missing*. Andrew Rice, age twenty-seven, last seen in Hamelin Bay. The article went on to describe Rice as a small-time drug dealer with a criminal history that included car theft, trespassing, and possession with intent to sell. Reading between the lines, it was clear. In spite of Andrew Rice's mother's impassioned plea for information on her son's whereabouts, the piece implied the man's disappearance was drug related. The accompanying photograph showed a young man, his face unsmiling and intense with a clearly visible snake-head tattoo curling its way up his deeply tanned neck.

Lucy leaned back in the chair and focused her eyes on the ceiling where a yellowish water stain spread across the paint work like a poisonous cloud. The three men, Whelldon, Jacobs and Rice, shared similarities, not only with each other but with Tim. The fact that they were in Damon's file told her the men hadn't been found. And, while each disappearance could be contributed to the dangers of the men's lifestyles, Lucy couldn't ignore the possibility that there was a link between the type of victim and the region where the men disappeared.

She returned her attention to the folder, flicked through the papers and pulled out the map. Unfolding it on the desk, she traced her finger over the red lines Damon had drawn, connecting Night Town with Busselton, Gracetown and Hamelin Bay. All three towns were within a couple of hours' drive of Night Town with Gracetown being the closest at about a thirty minute drive and Hamelin Bay being the most distant at an hour and a half.

There was something here. Something sinister. She could almost feel it in the way her skin prickled as she stared at the map. The more she studied the red lines, the more the pattern reminded her of a spider's web. Could it be possible that all three men ended up in Night Town? And if they did, what happened to them?

She pushed back the chair and stood, arching her back and rubbing at the base of her spine. With Tim *and* Aidan missing in town, how big a jump was it to assume there was a predator operating in the area? Was she seeing patterns that didn't exist just because she wanted...? No, she corrected herself, not wanted – *needed* – to find a trail that would lead to her brother.

Standing and staring at the map wanting the answer to somehow materialise, the rattle of the door opening made her jump. Damon entered with a plastic carrier on one arm and a brown paper bag wedged under the other.

He glanced over at the open folder. "So, what do you think?" He moved around the room, pulling a bottle of whiskey out of the paper bag and setting it on the nightstand. He dropped the carrier on the bed.

"I think you might have a career as a journalist. I'm impressed with your research." She didn't know why she was deflecting the question, only that suddenly, she wasn't sure if she wanted Damon to be right or wrong about what was happening in Night Town.

Damon frowned and opened the carrier. He pulled out a package of paper cups. "Is it too early for a drink?"

Five minutes later they sat outside on plastic chairs, facing the small garden at the rear of the motel. The area was decorated with a few benches and a cracked bird bath. To the left, beyond a thicket of hedges, Lucy could hear the sound of traffic as vehicles entered and exited the town.

She held a paper cup between her knees while she took a cigarette out of the battered packet. "Is it possible..." She spoke around the cigarette, "...that the missing men have absolutely nothing to do with Tim and Night Town?"

"Anything's possible." Damon sipped his whiskey, watching her over the rim of the cup. "But it's also possible that those guys and Aidan *and* Tim all disappeared here." He jerked his thumb over his shoulder.

Lucy lit her smoke and nodded. "It's spooky as hell looking at those articles and comparing the men with Tim, I'll give you that. But is it enough?"

The breeze ruffled his dark hair, lifting it from his forehead and exposing the smooth skin underneath. "That's why we need to keep digging. My gut tells me something is off in this town and if we ask the right questions of the right people, we might find out what lies under all this hostility."

"You've got the hostility part right." She thought about the librarian and the way the woman's mouth dropped open when she caught Lucy watching her on the phone. Damon was right about something being off about the place.

For a few moments they sat in silence. Lucy puffed out a long stream of smoke and chased it with a sip of whiskey, enjoying the way the liquid slid down her throat like a silky wave. The grass was still damp from the afternoon rain shower; the dewy smell reminded her of winter mornings and the promise of a fresh day. Now she wondered if that promise was an illusion. She'd lost so much in her life, would another day mean another loss?

She took another sip from the paper cup and tried to hold onto hope. Hope that Tim was still alive and that she'd have the strength to find him. Glancing over at Damon, she caught him watching her. Rather than look away, he held her gaze.

"You surprise me." It was an odd thing for him to say, but she was glad of the change of subject.

"Why? Because I smoke and drink whiskey?" She could feel a smile tugging at the sides of her mouth when only a moment ago she'd been close to another bout of crying.

"No." His amber eyes, so like the liquid in her cup, sparkled. "But I do like a woman who drinks whiskey."

"Do you?" She was laughing now, the warmth of the whiskey spreading through her chest like a calming balm on ragged nerves.

"What surprises me is your tenacity. When you didn't get the help you needed from the cops, you jumped in your car and came here to find your brother on your own." He looked into his cup and swirled the liquid before continuing. "On the drive here you told me about the barmaid, the librarian and the cop. In the face of that much enmity, most people would have turned tail and run." He gestured to the motel behind them. "Yet here you are even in the face of something as horrifying as, well..." His eyes lost their sparkle. "Well, I'm surprised you're still here."

Like the last few raindrops clinging to the wilting plants in the motel garden, her brief moment of good humour was trickling away. She dropped the cigarette onto the damp grass and squashed it under her boot.

"I'm not going anywhere until I find Tim." Her sorrow and despair was hardening, turning into something solid and immoveable. "I don't care if everyone in town lights a torch, grabs a pitchfork, and bangs on the pub door." She drained the last of her whiskey. "Now...you mentioned asking the right questions of the right people."

She stood and rubbed her hands together. "I have a few ideas."

Chapter Seven

It was almost eight p.m. when Damon walked Lucy to her car. The moon was out, but dark clouds crowded out most of the glow. As she opened the driver's door she stopped and, for a moment, a streak of slivery light fell on her face. In that instant, watching the now-familiar curve of her lips, he found it strange that they'd only met the day before.

"I'll pick you up at eight o'clock tomorrow morning." She stood with one arm draped on the car door. "That will give us time to have breakfast and formulate our plan of action."

"Sounds good." He could smell whiskey on her breath, the scent an alluring mix of cloves and toffee. He clamped his hands behind his back and fell into a habitual pose. "I'll be ready."

She turned to enter the car, but stopped. "Thank you, Damon." Her voice was soft, a little more than a whisper.

"For what?" The colour rushed to his face, making him grateful for the gloom.

"For doing this with me." She looked down at the grey of the parking lot. "I know you think I'm this tenacious reporter, but I'm grateful that I *don't* have to do this alone."

He felt a jolt; a hot sensation in his gut that he recognised as guilt. Sharing the information he had with her had drawn her deeper into whatever was going on in Night Town. If he'd said nothing, continued to play dumb, she might have given up and gone home. But he'd dangled hope in front of her and now whatever happened would be on him.

"You're helping me as much as I'm helping you." The words tasted disingenuous on his tongue. Maybe he was helping her, but at the same time he was using her to help him find Aidan, to help him salve his own guilt.

As he watched the Saab's tail-lights disappear into the night, he hoped he was doing the right thing. *When did that ever stop me?* He'd always taken whatever steps were necessary to get the job done. Even if it meant ordering kids like Aidan to do things that ate away at their minds until they ended up in a place like Night Town.

He ran a hand over his chin and continued to watch the road long after Lucy's car had been swallowed by darkness. Finding Aidan was supposed to be a chance at redemption, but here he was using Lucy to help him get the job done. If anything happened to her, he wouldn't have the luxury of hiding behind doing his duty this time.

* * *

By the time Lucy climbed the stairs at the back of the pub her limbs were heavy with exhaustion. There was a single light burning on the second floor, leaving much of the upstairs walkway in shadows. Snatches of music drifted up from below as the door between the lounge and back stairs swung open.

Lucy moved as quickly as her tired body would allow, unlocking the door to her room and slipping inside. She thought about setting up her laptop and sending some notes to her office email, but discarded the idea in favour of putting on her pyjamas and crawling into bed.

As she pulled on her nightclothes her mind returned to the things she'd seen in Damon's file. While the articles and map gave black and white information, she couldn't shake the feeling that she'd been looking at something else in those pages. A malevolent presence who'd managed to operate in secrecy and with a certain amount of freedom. Could that freedom come from the town itself? It was a question she'd posed to Damon.

"I guess we'll find out tomorrow." She spoke to the empty room, her eyes fixed on the dark window pane.

There were so many questions and, so far, few answers. Her mind couldn't move past the pictures of the missing men and the spider's web of lines leading to Night Town. And then there was Damon. Her gut told her to trust him, but things were shifting between them and her feelings for him were becoming something more. She rubbed the corners of her eyes with the tips of her index fingers. Lucy wasn't quite sure how to describe her relationship with Damon, and the uncertainty made her chest constrict with anxiety.

She'd only ever had one serious relationship. One man she'd allowed to get close to her, the only man she'd slept with. And that brief twelve months of happiness had come to a painful end three years ago. Since then she'd focused on work and had been not happy, but almost content.

She pulled back the covers and climbed into the double bed. Her mind needed rest, time to reshuffle, maybe organise the information swirling around her thoughts. Before turning off the lamp beside the bed, Lucy set her phone alarm for seven a.m. and placed it under the lamp.

In the darkness she focused on the narrow bar of light under the door coming from the landing, and let her eyes close. Despite the maelstrom of emotions she been through that day, her thoughts settled quickly and in seconds she was asleep.

A transferral of air accompanied by a whisper of movement brought her awake. For an instant she was confused by her surroundings and then the light under the door came into focus. Something woke her, but what it was and where it came from was unclear.

Fully awake now, eyes wide in the dark, she sat up and scanned the room. Seeing only dark shapes, she held her breath and waited. The sound came again, like someone breathing through a funnel, and then a metallic *clink*; a sound so soft it was barely audible. Lucy's heart jumped then fluttered. Unsure if there was someone in the room, she reached out meaning to turn on the lamp then hesitated.

Her eyes were adjusting to the gloom, bringing shapes into clearer focus. Unless someone was crouched next to the bed, she could see nothing out of place. *Why did I have to think about someone crouched near the bed?* Her hand, still outstretched, trembled. She snatched up her phone and checked the time: 12:08. Afraid of what she might see and even more terrified of continuing in darkness, she turned on the light on her phone. The blue glow bathed the bed in a cool arc.

Swallowing a dry lump that had formed in the back of her throat, she leaned left and played the light around the bed. The area was clear and the room silent. Almost convinced she'd been awakened by the sound of the old building settling, she crawled forward onto her knees and began directing the light to the right of the bed.

Finding nothing but an aging mat and bare jarrah boards, she let out a relieved breath. As the air escaped her lips a *clink* followed and this time the scrape of metal on metal. She froze. Propped up on her knees in the middle of the bed, phone light still on, Lucy stared at the door.

The light beneath the entrance to her room looked wrong – cut off in the middle. She clamped her teeth together and watched as the bar of illumination moved. *Oh, Jesus.* Someone was at the door. The shape, now clearly a person, moved again. A trickle of sweat, cold and sudden, broke out on the back of her neck. Her first instinct was to scream, but the saliva in her mouth evaporated, leaving her lips and tongue dry. If she tried to call for help and mustered only a croaking shriek, whoever was at the door would hear her. Would the sound be loud enough to bring help or just enough to force the would-be intruder to act?

Lucy slid to the left, trying to minimise any sound, and stepped off the bed. Moving on the balls of her feet, she headed for the desk near the far wall. As she crossed the room the *clink* became a rattle. Picking up the pace, she set the phone on the desk so the light was pointed at the door, and picked up the chair, wincing at the creak of wood as the shadow moved under the door.

Hurrying now with the chair held in front of her, she approached the door. As the knob began to turn, she dumped the chair and wedged the backrest under the knob, halting its rotation. She let out a gasp and stepped back, her shaking arms almost out of control.

The knob rattled with more insistency and the door shook in its frame. Lucy, still backing away, struck the desk and sent the phone spinning. She fumbled the mobile to a stop and snatched it up. Her mind turned slowly like wet cement as she tried to focus on her next move. The door knob shuddered and the chair shifted.

"Oh shit. Shit." Lucy's first thought was to call the police, but in a small town, the station was most likely closed or unmanned at this hour. "Damn."

She kept her eyes trained on the door, snatching quick glances at the phone as she scrolled through her contacts. At last she found what she was looking for and made the call.

The sound of ringing seemed distant and faint like the recipient was on the moon and not close by. The door shook this time with more force. Whoever was outside her room no longer cared about waking her. There was anger in the way the knob twisted and the wood shook, a ferocity that made Lucy wanted to scream.

"Come on." Her voice was a small squeak of desperation. Finally, after what seemed like minutes, the call connected.

"Hello?" Angie answered, her voice husky with sleep and surprise.

"This is Lucy." She was having trouble forming the words as her breath whooshed out in frightened bursts.

"Who?" Angie sounded angry now. "Who is this? Do you know wh—"

"It's Lucy Hush in room four. Someone's trying to break into my room." She was panting now that the words were out. The roar of blood in her ears made it difficult to hear Angie's response. "I need help."

The rattling stopped, but the shadow of feet at the bottom of the door remained. "I've called for help!" This time her voice worked and the threat came out as a half-scream. She took a step away from the desk and towards the door. "Someone's coming!"

Somewhere downstairs a door slammed, and the feet caught in the bar of light at the bottom of the door moved and were gone. At least Lucy hoped they were gone. Taking a few more steps, she reached the door and leaned over the chair so her ear was close to the wood. Heart still pounding, she tried to narrow her senses and pick up any sound of movement.

The pub and upstairs accommodations were quiet. Apart from the roaring pulse in her ears, she detected no sound. A shiver ran down her back, not one of fear, but more like a rush of weakness as the adrenalin ebbed in her system. Still in mostly darkness, Lucy closed her eyes.

The wood sprang under a blow powerful enough to bounce her face off the door. Lucy screamed a full-blown cry of terror and jumped back.

"Open up. It's Angie."

Lucy huffed out a sound that was a mixture of relief and surprise and pulled the chair away. The door opened and the barmaid, face scrubbed clean of make-up and wearing a fluffy blue robe, stood on the landing.

"What's going on?" Angie's wide face looked pale and shadowy under the walkway light. "I thought someone was being murdered up here." She sounded shaken and disgruntled at the same time.

Lucy, realising her room was still in darkness and reached for the light switch next to the door. "There was someone trying to get in." The room sprang into light, making Lucy squint and take a step back. "He was trying to force the door."

Angie took an exaggerated look both ways and shook her head. "There's no one here now. Are you sure you weren't dreaming?" There was an edge to the woman's voice: impatience and disbelief.

Lucy opened her mouth to answer, biting back a shriek of indignation. "I wasn't dreaming and I know what I heard."

"Why was your door unlocked?"

The question took Lucy by surprise. Rather than being concerned, Angie was blaming her. "It wasn't. I locked it before going to bed."

"Well, it was unlocked when I tried it." The woman was clearly angry now.

Lucy let her head tip back and look up at the ceiling afraid that if she continued to stare into Angie's obstinate face she'd lose control and say something she'd regret.

Angie must have sensed her frustration because her next words were a little less accusing. "Look, just lock your door and go back to bed. There's no one here."

Lucy lowered her gaze and fixed her eyes on Angie. She had the pasty skin of a woman that was never without heavy make-up. Beyond the washed-out appearance there was something else. If Lucy hadn't been so freaked out when the woman first appeared, she would have recognised fear in Angie's eyes.

"Do you know who was at my door?"

The question caught Angie off guard.

"No. Of course not."

Lucy noted the woman's rapid blinking and sudden shift in stance. She was lying.

Lucy held her ground and, as she expected, Angie broke eye contact and looked away. "I can't stand here all night." The protest was half-hearted, an attempt to redirect the moment and rescue her position as the one in control of the situation.

Lucy nodded. "Give me five minutes."

* * *

Damon started awake as pounding rang out in the darkness. For a split second, somewhere between sleep and wakefulness, he reached for his gun only to find the pale motel sheet bunched in his fist. The pounding continued, the racket jarring in the small room.

Scrambling for light, Damon swung his legs over the side of the bed. The cheap digital alarm clock read 12:42. In the ten seconds it took to check the time and switch on the lamp he was fully awake. Rather than rush to the door, he side-stepped the bed and reached into his pack and retrieved a twenty centimetre piece of steel pipe.

Before opening the door he stood to the side of the window and inched the curtain back. The figure at the door was little more than a dark shadow, one arm angled down and slightly back from the body suggesting it was holding something. Damon scanned the parking lot but couldn't see anything out of place.

He let the curtain fall back in place and put his hand on the door knob. There was another knock. Damon tensed his body and pulled the door open, hoping to catch his late-night visitor off guard while the person's hand still knocked on the door.

"Lucy?" He couldn't keep the surprise out of his voice.

Wearing a coat over blue pyjamas, she stood in the shaft of light spilling out of the open door. The startled look on her face turned Damon's surprise to concern and then embarrassment as he realised he was wearing nothing but a pair of black boxers.

"I didn't have anywhere else to go." She smiled, but there was no happiness in the expression. "I hope it's okay." She let go of the handle of her suitcase and pushed a tendril of chestnut hair off her cheek. "I just need somewhere to crash until morning." She rubbed her palms together. "I um… I can sleep in my car if it's too much of a bother, but…" She trailed off and glanced over her right shoulder.

"No. I mean… it's fine." He realised he was still blocking the entrance and stepped aside, the pipe held behind his back. "Come in."

She wheeled her little red suitcase into the room and stood near the bed. "I'm sorry to turn up like this, but I couldn't stay at the pub." She had her back to him, but the tremor in her voice told him she was struggling to keep her emotions under control.

He wanted to put his arms around her and tell her it was okay, that whatever had happened he'd take care of her. Instead, he grabbed his T-shirt off the end of the bed and pulled it over his head, tossing the steel pipe where the shirt had been.

"Don't apologise. Just sit and tell me what happened."

He waited as she unzipped her coat and sat on the bed. Her eyes, as they darted around the room, reminded him of the calla lilies his mother kept in a pot on the kitchen table: rich and smoky green.

She let her hands drop into her lap and for the first time since he met her, Lucy looked afraid. Not shaken up as she had been after hitting the fox, or grief stricken over her brother, but frightened. She was doing her best to cover it up, but he could see fear in the way her hands shook and her gaze danced between the window and door.

She jerked her chin at the pipe. "Jesus, Damon. Who were you expecting?"

He shrugged and, catching himself in the dismissive response, stopped. If there was danger, it was time for him to be honest with her. "I honestly don't know." She seemed unsurprised by his response. "We're asking questions that, for whatever reason, people in this town don't want asked. I like to be prepared." He could see by her reaction that she understood at least in part what he was talking about.

He sat down beside her and took her hand; it felt small and cold, so he covered it with his other hand, enclosing it in his grasp. "Now, tell me what happened."

Damon listened as Lucy recounted what happened at the pub and the barmaid's reaction. When she finished he got up and, using a couple of fresh paper cups, poured them both a shot of whiskey.

"Do you think it was just a pissed off local at my door or…" She hesitated so he finished for her.

"The guy who took your brother and the others?" He handed her the cup and sat on the edge of the bed.

She stared into the cup without speaking. Damon wondered what was going through her mind. Was she grappling with the gravity of their situation or wondering if she should call it quits and leave?

"It's good you're here." He nudged her shoulder with his. "Safer."

She looked up and gave him a smile, and for the first time since turning up at his door she looked calm. "I'll go to reception in the morning and book a room."

The ball of tension that had been building in his gut since she told him about the attempted break-in loosened and he realised the thought of her pulling out and leaving was more frightening than anything they might be about to face. Not because he needed her help, but because he didn't want her to vanish from his life before he had the chance to really know her. Lucy wasn't like any woman he'd ever met. She was strong and fiercely protective of her brother, but there was also a funny gentleness to her that was at odds with her choice of career. If he wanted her to stay and trust him, it was time to come clean. Completely clean.

"While I was looking for Aidan, I spoke to a man in Busselton." He started the story, deciding it was best to just put it out there and let her decide what she wanted to do. "He knew Aidan, but the guy was a bit of a low-life and he was sketchy about talking to me, so I gave him my number and told him to call me if he changed his mind."

Lucy was watching him now. There was an eagerness in her expression that pulled at his heart. "He called me this morning before I saw you." Damon took a sip of whiskey and let the hot fiery liquid hit the back of his throat. "That's why I called, but you were so upset…" He wasn't sure how to explain without hurting her.

"What?" Lucy's voice was low and guarded like she was expecting a blow. "Just tell me."

"He said before Aidan disappeared he had mentioned Night Town. Aidan said there was something major going down, something he could make big money off." Damon let out a tired breath. "The guy didn't come right out and say it, but he was talking about a drug syndicate."

"Oh." Lucy put the cup on the bedside table and clasped her hands between her knees. "So you think these missing guys got themselves involved in drugs and that's why they disappeared?" Could that be the thing that had attracted her brother to Night Town? She rubbed her hands together as if rolling something on her palms. "You think Tim was involved in drugs? Drug dealing?" Her eyes when she faced him were wide and clear. The fear Damon had seen earlier was gone, replaced by something hard and determined.

"I don't know. But I think it's probably best if, when you book a room, you get the one next door."

Chapter Eight

After a restless night, Lucy watched the first glint of sun fall through the edges of the cheap curtains. Lying in Damon's bed, his clean scent on the sheets, she wondered if Tim was somewhere close by. Could he see the sun? The pale light combined with the mournful cries of magpies in the nearby trees made her think of her parents. The last time they'd all been together, her and Tim with their mum and dad, seemed so long ago. A night with such happiness spiralling into tragedy in the blink of an eye.

She stretched and rolled over to watch Damon. How, she wondered, did he manage to look so comfortable sleeping on the floor? Flat on his back and breathing softly he looked younger and less intense. The things he'd revealed the night before weighed heavily on her. She knew Tim was no saint, but a drug dealer? He'd never get mixed up in something so low. But even as she tried to reassure herself, a worm of doubt niggled at her reasoning. How much did she really know about her younger brother's lifestyle? How much had she turned a blind eye to?

Seeming to sense her gaze, Damon opened his eyes, so Lucy made a show of snatching up her phone and checking the time. Thirty minutes later they were both dressed and ready for what she hoped would be a fruitful day.

"Do you think it's a good idea for you to turn up at the quarry?" Lucy stuffed her newly acquired room key into her bag and pulled out the cigarette packet, rubbing the crumpled packaging with her thumb.

They were leaving the Hodge Podge café after a rushed breakfast of eggs and toast. Damon stopped on the pavement and placed his hand over her fevered fingers as they picked at the cigarette pack. "I'll be fine. You just do your thing and meet me back at the crossroads."

His touch was becoming familiar, and with it a return of equilibrium. In a few short days, she'd come to depend on his steadiness to calm her jangling nerves. "I'm not worried about my part. Roving reporter is my go-to role." She took one last look at the package and dropped it back in her bag.

Damon let go of her hand. "One of the things that looms large in this town is the quarry." He took a quick look up and down the street, making sure no one was close enough to overhear. "That place employs half the town. The other is Samson Nightmesser, the town's benefactor." He lowered his voice slightly. "If something big – a major operation – has been set up in this place, either Nightmesser or someone at the quarry is involved, or at least someone there knows someone who *is* involved."

Lucy opened the driver's door. "That's what's worrying me."

When they reached the crossroad that split between the Nightmesser House and the quarry, Lucy pulled over but kept the engine running.

He jerked his chin at the dashboard clock. "It's nine-forty. See you back here in an hour." Damon climbed out of the Saab and pulled his pack off the floor, slinging it over his shoulder.

He was about to slam the door when Lucy leaned across the seat. There was a fine layer of mist hanging in the air, curling around the nearby trees like an altocumulus wave. Lucy wanted to tell him to be careful but instead fell back on humour. "If a man in a van offers you lollies, run." It was a silly joke she wished she could take back, but Damon smiled and nudged the door closed before she could think of anything more meaningful to say.

As Lucy pulled onto the road she caught a glimpse of him in the rear-view mirror, a lone figure swallowed up by the mist. How many of the men in Damon's file disappeared on this road? The idea of something sinister lurking in the forests nagged at her as she drove towards Samson Nightmesser's house.

The private road ran for a little over a kilometre before curving east and ending in a wide cul-de-sac. The house filled the semi-circle at the end of the road like a glowering giant. Pulling the Saab to the shoulder of the narrow stretch of bitumen, she turned the engine off and stepped out of the car.

She wasn't quite sure what she'd been expecting, maybe an old Queenslander-style building with a return bull-nose veranda and tin roof or, in keeping with the family's wealth, something modern and sleek. But the building at the end of the private road was unlike any she'd seen in a country setting.

The house, best described as rustic gothic, was set back from the road by a grey, crushed-gravel path and was perched high above a natural stone retaining wall that curved and undulated beneath the limestone and red-brick structure. A building flanked in mist like a medieval fortress, complete with a jutting wall tower and large arched windows, sat high over the road. To the left, a gravel driveway curved behind the building, shielding any vehicles from view. Judging by the aged look of the bricks, Lucy guessed the house was at least eighty years old.

Dressed in her puffer coat, black jeans and a deep blue jumper, she hoped she looked convincing as a freelance journalist. *I am a journalist*, she reminded herself. The only thing she had to convince Samson Nightmesser of was her cover story. If she could talk her way into the house, ask a few questions about the man's charitable work and his family's contribution to the town, she planned on putting Nightmesser at ease and then taking the interview in a different direction. Rattle the man and see what shook loose.

Lucy ran her fingers over her hair, smoothing a few stray strands caught by the morning breeze before crunching her way along the gravel path and climbing the wide stone steps leading up to the house.

The terrace was a confusing expanse of full-length windows and curved stone walls. It took her a minute or so to locate the door at the east of the building. In contrast with the aging facade, a sleek silver security monitor with a built-in speaker was set into the wall beside the heavy, dark wood door.

She pressed the button under the speaker and waited, the only sound being the light whistle of wind in the surrounding pines and karri trees and the twitter of birds enjoying the safety of the dense forest.

"Yes?" The voice was definitely male but strained like the owner was suffering with a cold.

Lucy leaned into the speaker. "Hello. I'm Lucy Hush, a freelance journalist. I was wondering if I could speak with Samson Nightmesser about his philanthropic work in Night Town." A long pause followed, filled with barely audible static. Lucy wondered if she'd made a mistake not phoning ahead and asking for an interview, but in her experience surprise calls were a better way at getting instant results.

She pulled back slightly and stared into the tiny black circle above the speaker, letting whoever was on the other end get a good look at her. A single female journalist was less intimidating than a crew. She tossed her head, flipping a length of hair over her shoulder, and smiled. She hoped the gesture was appealing and non-threatening. A harmless young writer trying to carve out a living, churning out puff-pieces about the history of the south-west. With the smile beginning to feel stiff, her lips felt like they were frozen against her teeth. Lucy let a couple of seconds tick by.

She was about to press the button again when the nasal voice broke out of the speaker. "Just a moment." The intercom clicked off.

A few seconds later the door opened and a tall, slightly-built man in corduroy trousers and a tan cardigan craned his neck in Lucy's direction. "Can I see some identification?" She recognised the voice from the speaker.

"Yes. Yes, of course." She scrambled through her handbag, wishing she'd thought to have her ID ready. "Sorry." She pulled her wallet out and slid out her Media and Arts Alliance card, not wanting to show him her Channel 12 ID and blow her cover as a freelance journalist.

She handed the man the card, noticing his thinning hair and sharp features. He held the plastic ID close to his eyes before looking up and checking her face against the photo. Lucy waited, her heart fluttering with a mixture of excitement and nervousness. Interviewing Nightmesser had been mostly Damon's idea. He thought that by talking to the most powerful man in Night Town she might be able to get a better picture of what was really going on in the place, although Lucy had an inkling the interview was Damon's method of keeping her out of harm's way while he visited the quarry.

"All right." The man in the doorway handed Lucy back the card and gave her a smile that didn't quite reach his eyes. "I'm Samson Nightmesser. I can spare a few minutes, but only a few."

"Thank you. That—"

"Come in. You're letting in the cold air." He stepped to the side and gestured for her to enter.

An odour, something chemical and sharp, hung in the air, the smell made stronger by the stuffy warmth of the hallway. Lucy glanced at the curious collection of artwork that decorated the foyer: paintings of various sizes in deep reds and skin tones. Nightmesser moved swiftly, leading her past a wide staircase and a series of closed doors, and into a large sitting room that was dominated by a stone fireplace. The hearth was empty and scarred black from long-dead fires, the heat obviously coming from some other source.

Nightmesser gestured to a patterned sofa beside a set of glass double doors. Lucy sat and pulled out her notepad, noticing another startling painting hanging over the fireplace. This one suggested the artist was looking down on his subject, focusing on the top of the model's head and the way the hair parted to reveal soft white scalp. The effect was quite unsettling, almost clinical.

"Now..." Nightmesser sat facing her in an aging, red armchair. "I apologise for forgetting our appointment." He rubbed the side of his temple. "It's been a very stressful time for me. My sister's quite unwell and I'm kept busy looking after her."

Lucy watched the man settling himself in the chair and tried to keep her face neutral. He obviously misunderstood her explanation or had in fact been expecting someone else. Either way, she intended to make the most of the situation and squeeze as much information out of Samson Nightmesser as possible.

"That's fine. I understand." She set the notepad on her knee. "You said your sister is unwell. Nothing serious, I hope?" In the articles about the Nightmessers, Lucy had seen nothing about a sister. Although the information was probably of no use, her natural curiosity wouldn't let her overlook this new bit of background on the family.

Nightmesser looked towards the window. "Serious in that she's quite debilitated. A birth defect, but not life threatening." He swiped at the leg of his pants as though swatting away a piece of lint. "Now." He looked back at Lucy. "I suppose you want some details on the upcoming fundraiser?"

Lucy had the urge to look at her phone and check the time, but forced herself to stay focused on Nightmesser. "Yes, please." She threw in an enthusiastic nod which seemed to please him.

Nightmesser spoke slowly, the nasal tone to his voice working on Lucy's nerves like a speck of dust trapped underneath a swollen eyelid. He liked to talk, but seldom made eye contact; his unusual voice constantly filling the room. It seemed Samson Nightmesser was sponsoring an upcoming fair organised by the town council to raise money for a new community centre to replace the one that was constructed in the late 1980s.

Only half-listening, Lucy wrote the word 'sister' on her notepad and underlined it. It wasn't until he mentioned the quarry that her interest piqued. "So, the quarry is part of Nightmesser Holdings?"

The question seemed to confuse him. He swiped at his pants and frowned. "Yes, of course." There was an impatient tone to his voice. "The quarry has been in the family for years." He waved a dismissive hand in the air. "Now as I said, the quarry will donate to the building fund and the rest will come from amounts raised through the fair."

"That's a lot of money for the quarry to donate, isn't it?" Lucy watched the man's pale, almost grey eyes as they darted around the room. "I mean a local fair wouldn't raise more than ten or fifteen thousand dollars." She held her pen over the pad. "What would you say the new community centre will cost?"

Nightmesser looked at his watch. "I couldn't say. Now I really should be looking in on my sister."

Lucy sat back, letting her head rest against the back of the sofa. "So, is it just you and your sister? No other family to help you?"

His mouth puckered slightly like the new line of questioning offended him. He leaned forward in his seat. "Yes. Just me and my sister. Now I–"

"I have a brother." She wasn't sure why she said it, just that something in the man's reaction to her question about the quarry and his sister set her journalistic senses tingling. "Do you get a lot of tourists in Night Town?"

"What?" He huffed out the word around a surprised laugh.

Lucy leaned forward. "Tourists, drifters, you know, people just passing through?"

There was a change in his demeanour, almost a shift in posture as the long-winded town benefactor disappeared and was replaced by a man that was alert and suspicious. "Why are you asking me about drifters?" He stood and pulled at the hem of his cardigan. "Which newspaper did you say you worked for?"

"I'm just trying to work out why a small town needs a new community centre when the existing one is less than thirty years old. Even in a big city that would be regarded as…" she paused for effect, "…extravagant." She was moving back and forth between questions now, keeping him off balance. "You mentioned a problem with drifters?"

"No. No, I didn't say they were a problem."

Lucy's pulse quickened. "So, you do get a lot of drifters?"

He opened his mouth to answer when a telephone rang, the sound echoing in the large room. "Excuse me." He gave her a hard look and for an instant Lucy caught something cold and almost savage in the man's gaze. "Wait here." He turned and left the sitting area through a narrow door at the far end of the room.

Lucy let out a breath and stood. Nightmesser was hiding something, just what it was she wasn't sure. If the phone hadn't rung, she might have managed to get a bit more out of him, but recalling the look he gave before rushing out of the room, she wondered if *she* might be the one who had had a narrow escape.

Taking a quick look towards the arch that led to the hall, she crossed the room and stood by the door Nightmesser had used. The sound of his muffled and rapid voice came through the wood. Lucy pressed her ear to the door, but could only pick up odd syllables. With nothing to gain by listening, she decided to grab the chance for a quick look around.

She started with the desk at the rear of the sofa, riffling through the few papers on the blotter. Finding nothing unusual, Lucy opened the top drawer. Letters all addressed to Samson Nightmesser, but nothing for the sister. Lucy picked up an envelope and turned it over. The return address was for a place called St Ruben's, an aged care facility in Busselton. Nightmesser said his sister was his only family, so why was he receiving mail from a nursing home? On impulse she stuffed the envelope down the back of her jeans and pulled her jumper and coat down.

With her heart thumping somewhere up near her throat, Lucy approached the painting over the fireplace. The colours were deep and rich, but the image was jarring in its angles. She leaned closer and inspected the signature: S. Nightmesser. The chemical smell made sense now. Paint thinner. Lucy didn't know why she hadn't recognised it sooner.

"You'll have to leave now." The voice caught her off guard, making her stumble forward.

Nightmesser had opened the door and re-entered the room without a sound. The cardigan was gone, and somehow he looked taller, as if he'd been stooped over when they first met.

"Okay." Lucy kept her voice even, but between the paintings and the home owner, she felt more than a little spooked. "This painting is amazing. You're a great artist, Mr Nightmesser."

He nodded. "My sister is the artist."

Lucy waited a beat, but he didn't elaborate. "All right. Thanks for your time."

His wintery eyes drifted to the painting and his lids drooped slightly like the image mesmerised him. In spite of the warm air, Lucy felt a chill on her skin, and the urge to get out of the house became almost overwhelming.

"Thank you." She headed for the hall. "I'll see myself out."

She was hurrying now, her boots thudding on the floorboards. The hallway walls were littered with more paintings. Lucy didn't stop to admire them, sure that they would be just as disturbing as the one in the sitting room. Instead, she kept her eyes on the front door certain that with each step Nightmesser's hand would fall on her shoulder, his fingers pulling her back into the depths of the old house.

When she reached the door, Lucy's fingers fumbled over the latch. *Keep it together.* She was losing her cool. Any minute now and she'd start screaming like a teenager in a slasher film. The latch turned and she pulled the door open, grateful for the gust of cold air on her face. The fresh breeze blew away the cloying chemical smell that filled her nostrils.

Hurrying down the steps, Lucy looked back at the house and noticed the curtain twitch in the upstairs window. She couldn't see the door from the last step, but wondered if Samson Nightmesser was still there.

She picked up her pace and almost jogged to the car. By the time she opened the door and started the engine her hands were shaking. *Jesus, this town's turning me into a nervous wreck.* As she pulled the Saab into a U-turn and the house shrank into the rear-view mirror, Lucy shuddered out a husky laugh.

"What a weirdo." Her voice in the empty car sounded small and uncertain. She glanced around and couldn't help feeling the trees were closer, leaning in on the narrow stretch of road.

She'd badgered Nightmesser with questions. Was it any wonder he'd appeared hostile? No, she corrected herself, not hostile, downright strange and creepy. But did creepy mean he was involved in a drug syndicate? It was a big leap, but the man's behaviour aside, the community centre fundraiser was bugging her. She made a mental note to check out the old building and see if the place was really in need of replacing, because it seemed a lot of money was being spent on the town's infrastructure. And, from what she'd seen, it was all coming from Samson Nightmesser.

As she approached the split in the road, Lucy spotted a dark four-wheel-drive pulling onto the track that led to the quarry. She slowed the car, giving the other vehicle time to disappear before pulling over and turning off the engine.

It was ten thirty. Damon had been gone less than an hour and she already had a tight ball of anxiety sitting in the pit of her gut. Things had got weird at Nightmesser's house. She hoped Damon was doing better at the quarry. But the image of him disappearing into the mist kept pushing its way to the forefront of her thoughts. Unable to sit still any longer, Lucy got out of the car and lit a cigarette.

Chapter Nine

The door opened, pushing a cloud of grit in Tim's direction. Even with the bar of dim light from the doorway he could only make out the woman's legs and skirt, made visible more by the small lantern she carried than any outside illumination.

He coughed and winced at the pain in his ribs. Tasting dirt on his tongue, he licked his lips, but rather than moistening them, his dry tongue only caught in the cracked skin and pulled open a scabbed-over wound. Ignoring the trickle of blood on his chin, Tim pulled himself into a sitting position.

The panic building in his chest when he heard the now familiar rattle of the lock ebbed. It was Samantha, his captor's sister. Not the faceless man. Not this time. Tim felt the urge to cry, but doubted his body could produce the moisture. Besides, the woman was skittish. If he got too emotional, she'd disappear for days and he didn't think he could last much longer alone in the dark.

"I've brought you some water and something to eat."

He watched her ankles as she settled herself on the bench. She was careful to stay out of reach as she lowered a paper bag to the flagstone floor and shoved it in Tim's direction.

"I wish it could be more, but..." She trailed off, her voice a hurried whisper.

"Thank you." Tim reached for the bag and gasped when he noticed his hand in the light.

His fingers were black and caked with dirt, the nails jagged and bloody. He pulled the bag towards him and an image flashed in his mind. A mangy dog, scarred and frightened, taking a scrap of food from a stranger's hand.

He tore open the bag and pulled out a bottle of water. The first mouthful tasted salty and metallic as the blood on his lips washed over his tongue. He took another swallow, the water soothing his throat and mouth.

"Don't drink too fast." Her dark-coloured pumps shifted on the gritty floor. "You'll be sick."

Tim grunted and set the bottle down beside the sleeping bag. The paper bag contained a sandwich wrapped in waxed paper and an apple. He made himself slow down, smelling the food first before ramming the bread into his mouth.

"I know you like ham, so I put plenty in there." She was nervous. He could tell by the way she stuttered out the words in her husky voice. "I wish I could do more, but..."

The first time she'd said, *I wish I could do more*, Tim had begged her to let him go or call the police. But his pleas terrified the woman, sending her running from the room. In the dark he couldn't really tell how much time had passed before she returned, but it was long enough for him to reach the edge of madness with hunger and thirst. He knew better than to start begging again. Instead, he merely nodded.

"I used to have a cat." Her voice was stiff like she was unused to communicating with other people. "His name was Mr Baggins, but my brother wouldn't let him in the house."

At the mention of the brother, Tim stopped chewing. His hands shook, so he set the sandwich down on the waxed paper, afraid if he continued to hold the bread he'd drop it onto the dirty floor. Not that that would stop him eating. He'd gobbled up a spider the day before, cackling like Renfield in an old Dracula movie. Or was it the day before that? He couldn't tell night from day in his small cell.

As his eyes adjusted to the light, Tim was able to see Samantha's lap and the way her hands remained clasped together, fingers stained with paint.

"Have you been painting?" He wanted her to talk to him. So used to wandering the forest and bush alone, Tim didn't think he was capable of craving another voice, a voice filled with, if not kindness, then something like concern. He needed to hear her speak almost as much as he needed food and water.

"Yes." The word was a breathless whisper. "I've been in my studio. I'm starting something new. It's hopeless really, but I love the feel of a brush in my hand. When I touch the canvas, it's like, like... I don't know... It's silly."

"It's not silly." He took a bite of the sandwich, savouring the last few morsels. "Tell me what it's like when you touch the canvas?" He was trying to keep her talking, dreading being left alone again, but another part of him really did want to know what she felt when doing something she obviously loved because although Samantha infuriated him, something about her also pulled at his heart.

"It feels like I'm touching a lover." Her voice was scarcely a whisper, hands wringing nervously in her lap. "I told you it was silly. What would someone like me know about love?"

"I'm not the person to answer that." Tim picked up the apple and tucked it into his sleeping bag, desperately wanting to sink his teeth into the sweet skin, but knowing he might need to make the meal last. "I've never been in love. But when I sleep under the stars, I feel…" He mulled over the image in his mind: the black expanse of soft night sky, stars like points of silver, and the smell. He felt a sob building in his chest.

She leaned forward, her upper body coming into the light. Tim's eyes were hazed with tears, making it impossible for him to see clearly. "What do you feel?" she asked. There was something almost hungry in her voice.

"I feel real," he said.

* * *

Damon stepped off the limestone track and tucked himself into the forest. Moving slowly, he walked parallel to the trail, staying in the shadows and moving between the trees. It was slower going this way, but the road was too exposed. He intended to approach the quarry on his terms and that meant only being spotted when he decided it was time. Experience taught him it was better to hold back and get a look at the layout before coming out in the open.

The undergrowth was dense. Small trees and ferns, lush from winter rains, slapped at his legs and waist. The national park abutted this part of the town, making it easy to wander for miles and become turned around. As he moved he kept the track in view, always keeping just out of sight. So far there had been no trucks or cars heading in or out of the quarry, but from what he'd seen in town there was a flow of tipper trucks bearing the Nightmesser name.

Almost on cue the rumble of a diesel engine eclipsed the birdsong. Damon ducked into the undergrowth and approached the road. About fifty metres ahead, the limestone track widened into a large bay where a tipper truck was parked with the trailer up. The quarry had to be over the next rise.

The truck he'd heard came into sight, but rather than another tipper it was a box truck, the sort with a tail-lift to help with unloading. There was no Nightmesser logo on this one, just anonymous white panelling. Damon frowned and watched the truck trundle to the left, avoiding the bay area.

He picked up his pace, his boots *humping* over the forest floor. When he was satisfied there was no one hanging around the bay area, he darted across the track and ducked into the foliage on the other side. The box truck's engine was still audible, but the vehicle was nowhere in sight. Damon paused and listened. The fading grumble was coming from the west. He pushed on, following the sound until it waned into silence.

The tipper truck made sense because of its rigid open tray designed for loading and off-loading loose materials, but the box truck was out of place at a quarry. The smaller, enclosed vehicle could be delivering food, drinks or tools, but if that was the case, why hadn't the driver entered the quarry?

Damon continued on, moving west and cutting deeper through the forest. The trees were tightly packed, giant growths standing over smaller trees and dense ferns. As he weaved around thick clusters of trunks breathing in the clean scent of pine, Damon couldn't stop his mind from summoning an image of Lucy, something that had been happening more and more over the past twenty-four hours. It seemed impossible that in such a short time she'd become an ever-present part of his thoughts.

He wanted to find Aidan; he needed to do one last thing for the young man who'd lost his innocence serving under him. If he could do this one thing, maybe he could sleep without dreaming of the faces of men who had their lives snatched away or decimated under his command. But now there was more. He wanted to find Tim so he could give Lucy peace, and if they were too late, at least closure.

He stopped and braced himself against a thick pine, listening for something over the chatter of birds and the soft hum of the breeze. His jeans were damp and clinging to his thighs. Fatigues would have been more suited to the job, but he'd promised himself he'd never wear them again. A stupid promise. With wet denim chafing his legs, he cursed himself for the pointless gesture.

He pulled up his jumper and used the T-shirt underneath to wipe sweat off his cheeks and forehead. A faint note stood out from the echo of bird songs. Just a snatch of sound, little more than a syllable, but enough to focus him in the right direction.

Another twenty metres and the sound of voices was clear if not the words. Damon dropped his pack and pulled out his phone. Switching it to silent mode, he shoved it back into the side pocket. Next, he opened the bag and pulled out the length of pipe which he stowed in the back pocket of his jeans. As he stood and turned to retrieve the pack, he noticed a cluster of feathers. Damon nudged the small mound with his foot, knocking loose a dusting of earthy feathers to reveal an owl, its beak open in death.

His heart was racing, the blood pulsing in his ears. It was a familiar feeling, an almost comforting bodily reaction to impending danger. He forced himself to breathe slowly and worked his limbs loose, shaking his hands and opening and closing his fists before stretching his neck left and right. Within seconds his pulse slowed.

The smell alerted him before he reached the clearing. A thick heavy odour hung in the air: urine mixed with something fruity and sweet. A few metres further, the trees fell away and light flooded the area. Damon huffed out a breath, surveying the expanse of tall, slender nettle-like plants with distinctive seven-fingered leaves. The rows stretched for at least a hundred and twenty metres *and*, judging by the smell, the marijuana crop was ready to harvest. This was the *something big* going down in Night Town.

A whistle, shrill and piercing, followed by voices drove Damon back to the cover a tree provided. He'd been spotted. It made sense that an operation as big as the one to the west of the quarry would have security. He ducked low and jogged back through the forest, praying they were a bunch of amateurs. Before he'd made it to the thicker growth, a twang fractured the air and a hunk of pinewood cracked like a whip to his right.

Damon dove left and crawled on his belly as another shot rang out. Amateurs or not they were armed *and* prepared to shoot. "Fuck." He spat out the word and crawled right then left, switching directions, the *ping* of the shot still ringing in his ears.

He could hear voices now, at least three closing in on him. He slipped his shoulders out of the pack and rolled onto his back and raised his chin. He could see them, one on the right about twenty-five metres back and two on the left. Their shadows were moving forward, dark shapes bobbing in and out of sight.

Damon snatched a look in both directions and, spotting a clutch of sapling pine surrounded by compact ferns and high grass, he rolled left and crawled under the foliage. With the pack at his side, he raised his hips to give himself room to retrieve the steel pipe. Once the heavy length was in his grasp, he clamped it to his chest and waited as the crunch of boots approached.

* * *

At eleven-thirty Lucy started the engine. Something was wrong. Very wrong. Damon should have been back almost an hour ago. He'd promised to call if he was held up. She could see no reason why he'd leave her waiting, not unless something had happened to him.

"Shit." She bit off the word and headed back towards town.

It had been a mistake to let him go to the quarry alone. Not that she had any control over what the man did. But she should have gone after him or at least waited near the quarry. "Damn."

Lucy drove through town. The buildings and people seemed sinister, like stage-dressing in some giant play where unsuspecting visitors dropped off the face of the world. She pulled up at a traffic light and noticed a woman standing on the corner with a stroller in front of her. At first glance it seemed like an ordinary moment. But then Lucy noticed the stroller contained a sack of dog food and the woman had a jagged scar running from one corner of her mouth – the pulled, twisted flesh making the woman look like she was grinning.

The light changed and Lucy floored the accelerator, desperate to put distance between herself and the surreal scene. A second later the wail of a siren caught her attention. Checking the mirror, she saw a police car behind her.

"I don't believe this." She clicked her tongue, pulled over to the side of the road and watched in the mirror as the police vehicle tucked in behind her.

She ran a hand through her hair and grimaced. Senior Constable Hooley or Hoosey, she couldn't quite remember his name, climbed out of the Holden Commodore and approached her vehicle. He took his time pausing to inspect her back tyres and then flipping open his infringement book. He moved with deliberate and practised slowness, intended, no doubt, to give the offender time to sweat.

Lucy rolled her shoulders back and raised her chin as she lowered the window. The last thing her frazzled nerves needed was another encounter with the truculent officer.

He positioned himself to the far right of the window, making her twist her neck in order to look at him. There was a slight pause before he spoke, time for her to fill the silence with banal excuses in a feeble attempt to avoid a fine. Lucy held her tongue and waited, determined not to be the first to speak.

His eyes, pale and almost colourless, regarded her with distaste. "Step out of the car, please."

She was surprised by his request but didn't let it show. Obediently, she opened the door and stepped onto the road. A blast of icy wind blew back her hair and almost snatched her breath away. The senior constable brushed past her and flicked his pen in the air in a 'follow me' gesture. She followed him to the front of the Saab without speaking.

"Can you tell me why you took off at the light like a bat out of hell?" His face reminded her of a scalded pig, all pink skin and loose cheeks.

"Yes." Lucy had no intention of trying to apologise her way out of a ticket. After the morning she'd had, a fine was the least of her worries. "I sneezed and my foot hit the accelerator." It was a lie. A good one, she thought, considering it was spur of the moment. And, judging by the way the officer's lips clamped together in a sullen pout, he did too.

They were well out of range of the police vehicle's camera. It struck Lucy that he'd walked her to the front of the vehicle and not the back for that very reason. If they weren't on the main street with cars constantly slowing to gape at them, she might have felt a little unnerved by his actions. *This is ridiculous.* She was letting the morning's events get to her, seeing menacing faces wherever she looked.

He nodded and moved so his back was to her car. She watched the officer, unsure of what he was trying to do until he began speaking. "You think you're pretty smart, don't you?" She opened her mouth to answer, but he didn't give her the chance. "If you had any sense, you'd get in your flash car and head back to Perth."

Her composure was slipping; she could feel her mouth dropping open but felt powerless to stop it. "I... Are you threatening me?" Her voice was a notch too high, making her sound younger and slightly childish. He shook his head and in that instant his name popped into her head. *Holsey.* His name was Holsey.

Senior Constable Holsey turned back towards the Saab. "I'm writing you up for speeding. I'll need to see your licence."

Lucy walked back to the driver's door on legs that were stiff and uncooperative. She retrieved her licence and gave it to Holsey, determined to keep any sign of emotion off her face. As the officer scribbled in his book, Lucy tried to imagine what Tim had felt in this desolate, unwelcoming place. Tim, a man whose gentle nature and friendly smile drew people to him, must have found something in Night Town that made spending time here worth braving the inhospitable locals. Could he have been involved in the drug scene?

"Oh." Holsey handed her the ticket and fixed her with a long stare. The winter skies shifting overhead with thin grey clouds were reflected in his washed-out irises. "Your rear left tyre's a bit worn. Get that checked."

Lucy forced a smile that she hoped looked more genuine than it felt. "Yes, I'll do that."

Before he turned away she saw a flicker of something in his eyes, maybe disappointment. Had he been hoping she'd become difficult and give him a reason to arrest her? Whatever he was up to, Lucy felt relieved when he climbed back in his car and pulled away.

Once back in her room at the motel, she pulled off her coat and began pacing. She'd left three messages and one voicemail for Damon and so far had no response. A sick feeling stewed in her gut as the worry built to a maddening pitch. She couldn't just hang around the motel and wait, but what could she do? If she went storming out to the quarry, would whoever took her brother hold up his hands and admit he had Damon too? Or would Lucy go the way of the men in Damon's folder? Would her disappearance become another scant article hidden in some corner of the Internet?

She rubbed her hands together; the skin on her palms dry from the cold. The obvious answer was to go to the police. Senior Constable Day seemed okay, but if she turned up to report another missing man only a day after the first she'd look like a crackpot. Or worse, a liar. And if Day did take her seriously, he'd tell her to wait and let him do his job. What then? Days would go by. She couldn't leave Damon to die.

She stopped pacing and stared out of the small window overlooking the parking lot. The afternoon sun was struggling to break through the clouds, casting weak shadows like slanted fingers on the bitumen. For the first time she let herself think of Tim's disappearance in terms of death. Whoever was taking drifters wasn't collecting them like a lepidopterist. The young men in the articles were dead. It would be stupid to think otherwise. She had to accept that Tim might be dead too. Her heart stuttered at the idea of never seeing her brother again, but she forced her thoughts to move forward. There might be time to save Damon.

She had to act and soon. She gripped the window ledge, the cheap aluminium frame cold under her hands. Who would be left to report her missing? She had no family, only…

An idea came to her. By going to the quarry she was walking into danger, but at least she could leave a trail.

Energised by the prospect of taking action, she opened her laptop and fired off an email to Matthew, her producer at Channel 12. Matt Price had worked in journalism in one way or another for almost twenty-five years. He was a man she trusted more than liked. And right now, trust was all that mattered.

Keeping the details to a minimum, she outlined the information Damon had shared with her, explaining that Damon, her companion, had now vanished. She hesitated over the term 'companion.' Companion sounded outdated and pompous, a word so at odds with Damon's laidback personality that she almost changed it to friend. *Are we friends? What the hell does it matter what I call him?*

She shook her head and finished the email: *I'm going to drive back to the Nightmesser quarry and look for answers. I'll get back to you by five p.m. If you don't hear from me by then it means I need help. I need you to raise hell.*

It was a dramatic way to end the email, but they were in the news business and drama was everything. Lucy hit send and prayed that Matt was checking his emails. Once it was done, a small fraction of calm returned and her thoughts cleared. She'd go back to the quarry and flash her ID around, ask questions about Damon. Maybe whoever was behind the missing men would do something rash and make a mistake that would expose them. *Or kill me.*

The idea of facing a killer alone set her heart off on another hopscotch of jumps. Before she could sort through her plan any further, her phone shrilled with an incoming call. Letting out a gasp, equal parts surprise and relief, she grabbed the phone from her bag and answered without checking the number.

"About time. I was going mad with worry."

There was a moment of hesitation, the sound of a breath being drawn in. "Miss Hush, this is Senior Sergeant Day."

The room seemed to shrink around her and a second of confusion stretched into an awkward pause. It wasn't Damon calling her to say he was okay. The disappointment overshadowed all other thoughts as she tried to grapple with the situation.

"I… Sorry. Hello." Lucy wasn't sure what she was saying. The words were just dribbling out in an incoherent trickle.

"I've found something on your brother." Day's voice was calm, almost cheerful. The mention of Tim acted as a mallet, smashing through her confusion and disappointment. At first the news set off a jolt of relief, but the emotion was swallowed up with panic. "Could you come to the station? There's something I'd like to show you."

"Is he... Have you found his body?" The last word stuck in her throat and came out as more of a croak than a word. If Tim was dead, she wanted to know now, not over a cup of tepid instant coffee at the police station. She gripped the phone tighter and clenched her jaw.

"No. Nothing like that." She could hear him breathing. "I have a lead on Tim's disappearance that I'd like you to take a look at." She heard something rustling on the end of the line, the sound of a page being turned. "Sorry if I frightened you." There was a pause and she realised he was waiting for her to speak.

Her mind was still processing Day's words: a lead on Tim. "That's great. Yes, of course." She noted the time on the phone's display. It was close to one o'clock. If she met with the senior sergeant now there would still be plenty of time to make a decision on going to the quarry. Any information on Tim might not just help find her brother, but could also lead her to Damon. "I can come in now?"

* * *

Day greeted her at the counter and led her through to his office. Lucy was relieved to see Holsey's desk unoccupied and couldn't help pitying the poor unsuspecting motorist who was probably on the receiving end of the senior constable's brand of traffic policing.

"Have a seat." Day indicated to the chair she'd sat in the previous morning. "After we spoke yesterday, I went through a few local businesses to check on CCTV footage." He sat and pulled the computer keyboard towards him and began tapping keys. "Surprisingly, there are more cameras in Night Town than I would have guessed." He glanced up from the screen and she noticed the frown lines she spotted the day before were smoothed out and replaced by a look of excitement.

Lucy felt a quiver of his enthusiasm like a physical thing, something that jumped across the desk and took hold of her. "Did you find footage of my brother?" She didn't try to control the eagerness in her voice.

"Yes." Before she could respond, Day held up a finger. "It's just a short snatch. Only a few seconds, but there's something I want you to see."

He tapped a few more keys and turned the screen so it was slanted towards her. The image was of a stretch of pavement beyond a shopfront window. Although there was no sign of Tim, Lucy's stomach fluttered with excitement.

"The time and date are stamped there." Day indicated to the right-hand corner of the screen where a series of numbers were displayed.

"The sixteenth of June." She read the date aloud. The day before Tim sent her his last text.

"Yes." Day tapped the screen. "As you can see, the time shows 4:08 p.m. This was taken late afternoon so that explains why the picture's a bit shadowy."

Lucy nodded but couldn't drag her eyes away from the screen. She could see a long shadow breaking onto the screen from the right, the greyish shape looping off the pavement and into the gutter. Without seeing the clip play she knew that grey patch on the screen was her brother's shadow. There was nothing in the shape that identified the approaching figure as male or female. A frozen blob of dark pixels, yet somehow she knew.

"Now watch." Day clicked the mouse and the picture began moving. A figure crossed the pavement and Lucy's heart thumped into her throat.

"That's him." She leaned forward, eyes trained on her brother as he halted almost directly in front of the camera's lens. It was Tim right down to the big pack strapped to his back and the old woollen beanie perched on his head. "It's Tim." For a fraction of a second he ducked his head and seemed to be peering in the shop window. His face was perfectly, if not closely, framed. "Oh my God. You found him."

"Keep watching." The note of tension in Day's voice told her there was more to this viewing than just identifying her brother on the clip.

Another shadow moved into view. This one came from the centre of the picture and was quickly replaced by a set of legs – male legs. Whoever had entered the shot had done so from the road. Tim's head turned and even without sound it was clear the person who'd approached her brother was speaking. She could see the way Tim turned and looped a finger into the shoulder strap, securing his pack to his shoulder. The movement was casual and familiar at the same time. She'd seen Tim stand that way a hundred times. Tim was speaking to the man on the road.

"Who's he talking to?" Her voice was a whisper, like she was asking herself the question.

"That's what I was hoping you could tell me."

Lucy strained, eyes fixed on the stranger's legs and shoes: camel-coloured boots with a black trim at the ankle. As the clip progressed, Tim turned further away from the camera and shrugged. The stranger stepped forward, his thighs coming into view. Lucy was holding her breath now, willing the man on the road to step into the frame. But instead, Tim shook his head and walked across the pavement and out of view. The stranger stayed where he was for a fraction of a second. She still couldn't see the man's upper body, but somehow she knew he was watching her brother walk away. And as quickly as the whole scene played out it ended with the stranger stepping out of view.

"Do you recognise anything about the guy on the road?" Day was speaking now, asking her questions, but Lucy's mind was still replaying the clip, and seeing her brother again shrug his shoulders. What had the man said? Her mind jumped back to the night in the pub when someone was at her door. Seeing that shadow fall upon her brother put her in mind of the faceless presence trying to get into her room.

"Miss Hush?"

Lucy looked up from the screen where the clip was paused. Day was waiting for an answer. She felt tired and her eyes heavy like she'd been staring at the screen for hours.

"Call me Lucy." She spoke without thinking. "I don't know who that man was. How could I?" She slouched back in the chair. "I could only see his legs." Maybe it was the excitement and hope dissolving, but now even speaking seemed too much of an effort.

Day leaned his elbows on the table and sighed. He sounded as tired as she felt. It occurred to her that he must have viewed a lot of footage to find that clip. He'd said there were more cameras in Night Town than he thought, so how many hours of footage had he watched since yesterday? She looked around the room only now noticing the empty coffee cup on the desk and the smell of burgers in the air.

"How long did it take you to find that clip?" She surveyed Day's rumpled uniform.

He took his time before answering. "A while... So, the man in the clip wasn't a friend of your brother's?" He dodged the question with one of his own. "Someone he might have been meeting in town?"

Lucy thought of asking how long a while was, but Day had obviously put in hours trying to find something on Tim. The senior sergeant had done more to help than any other cop and he seemed genuinely disappointed that the guy on the footage wasn't identifiable. She wondered how Day would react if she told him about Damon. If she mentioned the attempted break-in at the pub, would he want to keep her under watch? The thought of having Senior Constable Holsey parked outside her motel room set her teeth on edge.

Lucy shook her head. "No. Not that I know of." He looked deflated. "Tim didn't have many friends, not many that he ever introduced me to." She was about to say more, ask where exactly the footage came from when her phone pinged with an incoming message.

Day's eyes travelled from her face to her bag. "Aren't you going to check that?" His voice was tight, overly casual.

Lucy managed a weak smile and pulled the phone out of her bag. She glanced at the screen and her pulse quickened. It was a message from Damon. She stuffed the phone back in her handbag and forced her face into a casual pose. "Work."

Day nodded. "Problems?" He was watchful now. In spite of the dark shadows, his eyes were keenly trained on her.

"Not really." She stood, eager to get out of Day's office and read Damon's message. "Just the usual stuff."

Day gave her a tight smile and rose. "I was hoping we had something with that clip. But don't worry." He spoke as he opened his office door and led her through the empty station. "I'll keep at it and see what comes up." He paused at the station's front door. "Will you be in town much longer?"

Lucy was having a hard time concentrating on what he was saying. Damon was okay and all she wanted was to see him and find out what happened. "Um... Yes, for a while longer." She wasn't sure how to finish. Until you and I find my brother was the answer, but she wasn't supposed to be interfering in the investigation. "A week at least."

They were at the front of the station now and Lucy had one hand on the exit. "Thank you for all you're doing, Senior Sergeant. It means the world to me that you're taking this seriously."

Day's face, usually unreadable, relaxed, and for a moment a smile lifted his features, making him look younger and less hardened. "Call me Brock."

"All right, Brock." Lucy pushed the door open and stepped out onto the pavement. Worried that Brock would be watching from the front door, she didn't dare check her phone until she was back in the car.

The interior of the car was only slightly warmer than the chilly air outside. Lucy pulled the phone out of her bag and read the text: *I'm walking back now. Can you pick me up near the bridge? D.*

There was a bridge on the far side of town, an ancient-looking wood and concrete structure that crossed a gully where the river rushed through the outskirts of Night Town. It was the only bridge she remembered seeing anywhere near town, so she guessed that's where Damon meant.

Lucy started the car and pulled out of the parking lot adjacent to the library. Knowing Damon was alive set off a concatenation of emotions that clamoured for dominance. In the end it was relief tinged with joy that won. In spite of the fluttering in her stomach, this time she drove carefully, being sure to watch her speed. The last thing she needed was another encounter with Holsey.

Less than ten minutes later she crossed the bridge and the Saab bumped over a hump in the road and left Night Town behind. On the left there was a marshy looking patch of scrub. Lucy entertained the idea of parking on the pulpy looking ground, but almost immediately discarded it. If the car became bogged, she didn't like the idea of calling a local tow-truck. *Not in the town where friendliness goes to die.* She chuckled to herself and drove a few metres further down the two lane road and pulled off onto a patch of gravel.

She climbed out of the car to the sound of rushing water. It was a clean sound, one that made her think of the ocean and how her skin felt when the cold water lapped at her body. Maybe it was just being out of town and breathing air that wasn't contaminated by a sense of sullen resentment, whatever the reason, her mood was rising. For the first time in days she felt more than just anxiety.

Her boots crunched over the gravel then slowed in the boggy ground. A dark vehicle approached, heading out of town. She couldn't be sure but it looked like the one she'd seen at the quarry that morning. As it drew closer Lucy turned away from the road and flipped up her hood. Unable to see the four-wheel-drive, she listened to the engine and noted a decrease in revs. Was it slowing?

She stepped across the muddy ground, her shoes sinking into the soft earth. She waited, blood pounding in her ears and blocking out the rush of the river. If the vehicle stopped, she was ready to run into the bush. But the engine revved and the 4WD tore down the strip of bitumen, leaving a plume of white steam clouding the road.

Had the car really slowed or was it her frenzied mind? She flipped back her hood and wiped her lips with the back of her hand. Maybe she should have told Brock about what happened at the pub. Keeping everything to herself had always been her first instinct. Maybe that's why journalism appealed to her. In some ways it was a selfish, lonely profession where the more you guarded information the better chance you had of breaking a big story. But this wasn't a story; it was her life and the lives of others – Tim's life.

She looked back towards town and caught movement on the embankment leading to the river. A shape emerged from the base of the bridge. Lucy squinted and watched as a familiar figure stepped up to the scrubby area near the road. Nerves still twanging, she hesitated, making sure what she was seeing was real.

Lucy let out a rush of air and started forward, her coat flapping out behind her. The urge to run almost got the better of her, but she let her muddy boots keep her at a moderate pace. Damon drew nearer and dropped his pack to the ground. No longer caring if she was being dramatic or overstepping their friendship, Lucy broke into a jog and didn't stop until she ran into his arms.

Damon let out a gasp as she nearly toppled them both back down the embankment. She wrapped her arms around his back and pressed her face into his shoulder. "Damn it, Damon. Y-you s-scared ten years off my life." She was stammering, but didn't care.

His arms came around her and his hand was on her hair. "Sorry." He smelled earthy as if he'd been rolling around in wet grass. "I found something, but let's get off the road first. I'm not sure how safe it is out here."

She nodded into his shoulder, her cheek brushing the cold leather. Reluctantly, she let him go. "Okay. Come on. It's freezing." She stepped away from him only now noticing the state of his clothes. "You're wet."

"Yeah." He took her hand and pulled her towards the car. "I'll tell you everything once we get back to the motel."

Chapter Ten

The light came on, flickering at first and then settling to a dim yellow glow. Tim sat up and gasped. The pain in his ribs was spreading. It raged across his torso. The light, no matter how weak, stung his eyes. He remembered reading somewhere that prolonged periods of darkness could damage the eyes. Not that it mattered. He doubted long-term damage was his problem. Not anymore.

Without knowing the time or if it was day or night, it was almost impossible to predict how regularly the lights would burst to life. If he had to guess, he'd say twice a day.

As he'd done other times, Tim rubbed his eyes and looked around the room. *Cell, not room.* The walls were old, made of uneven stones and packed tightly with rough mortar. Despair, like a grey shark, circled his thoughts as he took in his grim surroundings. The ceiling was high, at least three metres. Even if he did have some way of reaching it, the single bulb was enclosed in mesh and the ceiling a network of dark heavy beams filled with some sort of fibro-cement.

His feet were secured with a pair of tarnished handcuffs; one cuffed around his right ankle, the other linked to a heavy chain bolted to the stone floor. To reach the small wooden long-drop toilet in the corner Tim had to hoist the chain, shuffle the two metres his restraints allowed, and stretch out his right leg. Then and only then could he relieve himself while crouched on one leg. A balancing act best accomplished with light.

Knowing the bulb could flicker off at any time, he made the journey to the toilet and relieved himself as quickly as his diminished strength would permit. The stench from the long-drop filled the small cell with a thick odour that saturated his every breath. Sometimes he imagined he was in hell and the unending pain and misery his punishment for surviving when his parents had lost their lives. *No*, he shambled back to the sleeping bag. *I don't deserve this.*

He was no saint, but his only real crime had been trespassing. Yes, he'd taken some weed and camped illegally, but did that warrant this unending torture? He sat on the sleeping bag and fixed his gaze on the door. There had been a few times in his life when he'd questioned his own sanity. More than a few. The weeks he'd spent in Graylands Hospital had been the worst. Psychiatrists and nurses treated him like he was a danger to himself. Hell, like he was a danger to others.

Tim remembered thinking he couldn't sink any lower. He let out a laugh, soft and joyless in the stone room. "I guess I was wrong."

He'd found a new low point in this room and he suspected there was worse to come. Samantha's brother, the nameless faceless monster that filled his nightmares, was always on the edge of Tim's mind. *When will he come back? How much will he hurt me? Will he kill me?* The questions pushed out every escape plan or notion of survival until Tim crumpled into a ball of desperation.

The lights cut out and blackness filled the cell. He could hear his own breathing, slow and solid in the darkness. Somewhere in the depths of the building a tap dripped, its regular *plop* like a nail being driven into his brain. Had the brother let the tap drip to torture him? He forced his mind to work on something outside the confines of the room. Something he could visualise.

He slowed his breathing and narrowed his thoughts until the night sky replaced the blackness; dark, yet not a dull void like the room. Tim saw an expanse of rich deep grey overlaid in silky translucent black. A space where stars ruled over jagged treetops, their polished glow like fingers of light. He sucked in a breath and could almost feel the cold wind filling his lungs.

"It's worth living for." The whispered words reminded him of something Lucy once told him.

The sky was replaced by his sister's face. Smooth, clear skin framed by impossibly shiny brown hair. Her wholesome prettiness out of place in the hospital ward. Lucy sitting beside him, listening patiently to his complaints. When he was done whining like a spoiled brat, she nodded, seemingly in deep thought.

"I'm sick of hearing how shitty your life is." Her words took him by surprise. He'd come to rely on her endless sympathy; this new Lucy startled him out of a muddy pond of self-pity. He remembered trying to stumble out a protest, but she shook her head, hair bouncing on her narrow shoulders. "There *are* plenty of reasons to die, but you only have to find one..." she held up a finger, "...just one good reason to live. Something worth living for. Do that." Lucy waved her hand at the comings and goings of the other patients and staff. "Everything else melts away."

"Everything else melts away." He repeated the words to the empty room.

She was right. He smiled into the darkness. She usually was. After that day he'd focused on what made his life worth living and trampled the reasons to die. Lucy saved him, not the doctors or the medication, but his big sister's words. She was a warrior, an old soul born into a modern world. He choked back the tears trapped like a ball of wire in the back of his throat. Lucy would fight, not lie down and cry.

A door whispered open, its distant whoosh overly loud amidst the limited sounds. Tim cocked his head to the side and listened as light appeared under the door. But instead of the clack of Samantha's heels, he heard the dull thump of boots.

Despite everything he'd promised himself, Tim's body tensed as terror ground its way into his bones like an orthopaedic drill. The fear twisting and turning until his limbs were numb. Using the wall for support, he forced himself to stand, determined not to cower this time.

The door rattled and swung open. In the feeble hallway light, he stood. Bare chest, smooth and hairless, arms hanging at his sides and hands encased in thick fingerless gloves. In one fist the camera, black and bulky. Tim tried to swallow but the saliva had evaporated, leaving his mouth like a dry husk.

The brother wore a mask, a joke shop veneer that covered his entire head in rubber. Designed to be funny, the old lady mask grinned a joyless smirk through a gap-toothed mouth, her jowly face topped with wild white nylon hair that fell in straggles over the latex monstrosity.

The masked man didn't speak, just stood, clenching and unclenching his fist as the camera dangled against his thigh. Tim looked past the man, straining to see into the hallway.

The night they brought him here he'd been dazed and semi-conscious. He remembered being torn from sleep and a pain so hot and agonising that his muscles twisted and contorted. As he was half dragged from his tent he caught a glimpse of two men, their faces hidden by dark ski masks. Tim recalled struggling as he was shoved into the back of a dark car. At one point someone hit him with something heavy and blunt. After that there were only snatches of images: the moon through the car window, its cold brilliance comforting and indifferent at the same time, a ceiling long and yellowed, and him prone on the floor being dragged to his cell.

His memories of the building were sketchy at best, but there was an image that lodged in his mind: a narrow hallway, the floor a dull matte red. At one end, the door they'd dragged him through, and then the long expanse of red. Glimpses of that floor were visible at the man's back. At the end of that bloodshot flooring would be the outside world. So close, but unreachably distant.

The masked man raised the camera and snapped a photo. The click and whir of the instamatic made Tim jump and squint at the same time. His captor held the photo, watching Tim's image appear on the shiny square, then dropped the photograph to the floor.

"Take off your shirt." The masked man's voice was flat and emotionless, at odds with his heaving chest and heavy breathing.

Tim rolled his shoulders and lifted his chin. Last time, the man punched and kicked him without speaking. Now it seemed there was a new aspect to the sick game. "Fuck you." He put as much contempt into the words as his dry mouth could muster.

Slowly, in no hurry, the masked man placed the instamatic on the floor next to the door. Tim watched the man's movements, knowing his show of defiance would bring pain, but not sure when and how much.

When his captor moved it was with an unexpected suddenness that took Tim by surprise. The first blow, a backhanded slap, knocked Tim's jaw back and his head hit the wall with a muffled crack. The pain was instant. He staggered, but managed to stay on his feet even as dark splotches swam in his eyes.

"Take your shirt off." This time the voice was raised, an edge of anger clear in each precise word.

Tim held onto the wall, the stench from the long-drop working its way into his throat, mingling with the dizziness like a putrid soup of nausea. "Fuck you." He huffed out each word, mimicking the man's precise way of speaking.

This time a kick landed on Tim's shin, the heavy boot carrying enough force to knock his foot out from under him. Tim hit the stone floor hard, rolling to the right, grasping his shin and biting back a scream.

The man stood over him and Tim could smell the rubber mask, a plastic stench that reminded him of a condom. "Take off your shirt."

Tim clutched his shin. The agony in his leg shot daggers of fire up his leg as far as his thigh. Tears were building in his eyes, and as much as he'd promised himself he'd stay strong, he let them run down his cheeks.

"Take off your mask, you sick asshole." Tim's voice was warbling now as snot and tears covered his face.

The attack he was expecting didn't come, instead more photographs. At least four clicks as the man checked each image before dropping it onto the pile. Finally, he put the camera down and continued his violence: first tearing Tim's shirt open and pulling it down around his waist, then delivering short jabs to Tim's torso and face, each with measured force, painful, but not too damaging. *He wants me to stay conscious and feel every blow*, Tim thought briefly as the effort of breathing became more and more difficult.

When the beating came to an end, the masked man was holding the wall himself, out of breath and sweating. Before leaving the cell, he picked up the camera and continued to photograph Tim from various angles, moving in to capture the tears and the welts.

* * *

When Damon emerged from the bathroom he had a blue towel wrapped around his waist. Lucy noticed the way the damp fabric was draped low on his hips and quickly looked away. On top of everything he'd told her about the marijuana field and the armed men, burgeoning feelings for a man she hardly knew wasn't something she wanted to deal with. Not right now anyway.

"I've been thinking about it and we should go to the police." Lucy kept her eyes on the window, watching the afternoon sunlight turn to a hazy gold now that the clouds had cleared. "Those men could have killed you. It's crazy to continue this on our own."

Damon sat next to her on the bed. The clean scent of soap and shampoo wafted off him. "They could have, but they didn't." He sounded tired. "If we go to the cops, they'll swarm that field and people will scatter. If that happens, whoever took Tim might get away or go underground."

She wanted to argue and come up with reasons why it was too dangerous, but beneath all her inner protests was a desire to keep Damon safe. She thought she'd lost him today and couldn't stand the thought of feeling that way a second time. Not with Tim gone.

"Okay." She didn't want to look at him. He was too close on the bed, his naked skin only centimetres from her shoulder. "What's next?" She stood and busied herself, checking her phone, not really taking in the text on the screen.

"Next," Damon began, "we get something to eat."

As Damon scavenged through his bag looking for something to wear, Lucy read the text.

> *Don't do anything crazy!!! This could be a huge story. I can have a crew there by midday tomorrow. Hold off on going it alone until they get there. I don't want you getting yourself killed. Matt*

The producer's gruff concern took her by surprise, although she suspected part of his warning was based on not wanting to lose her inside knowledge of what was shaping up to be a major story. She fired off a return text.

Crisis averted; Damon's turned up safe. Hold off on the crew for a few days. There's a couple of things we need to check out. Thanks, Lucy

She dropped the phone back in her handbag, hoping she'd bought herself a bit more time. If police involvement could send the guilty party underground, a media circus would end their chances of finding Tim forever.

They settled on fish and chips, which they ate sitting in plastic chairs in the motel's small garden. Lucy watched a lone galah dip its beak into the broken birdbath as she dipped her fingers into the nest of white paper in her lap and breathed in the delicious smell of vinegar and grease. It would be dark in a few minutes and then the town would settle into silence. Under the lone outdoor spotlight, the garden looked less shabby and more peaceful. Sharing meals with Damon was becoming a comforting routine.

"You said those guys at the field chased you down, but you got away. How did you manage to give them the slip?" She shoved a rapidly cooling chip in her mouth and waited for Damon to answer.

He wiped his mouth on the back of his hand before replying. "I wish I could say I used mixed martial arts and my cat-like climbing skills." He gave her a crooked smile, the half-crescent lift of his mouth appeared to be holding back a laugh. "But the truth is I hid in the bushes for an hour. When I was sure they were gone, I crawled out and ran like hell."

Lucy couldn't stop herself laughing around a mouth full of chips. "Smooth."

Damon joined in the laughter. "I have been trained by the Australian government so I'm pretty stealthy."

Even as they both joked about what happened, Lucy had the feeling Damon was playing down his escape. When he showed up at the bridge his clothes were filthy and there was a scrape on his knuckles that was turning into an angry welt. But it felt good to laugh again, like something dark that had been covering the sky now drifted aside, letting in the light. She didn't know how long the feeling would last, but for now it was enough.

"So..." Damon finished crunching his way through a piece of fish. "Tell me what happened with Nightmesser?"

With everything that had taken place since leaving Nightmesser's house, Lucy really hadn't time to pick over the strange meeting. But now as she recounted the conversation to Damon, she felt a sliver of discomfort thinking about Samson's eyes and the way they changed from vague and pompous to almost vulpine.

"There's something strange going on there." She screwed up the paper, scrunching the few remaining chips with it. "Nightmesser's odd... He's really weird. But the part that got me thinking was all the new buildings. A lot of money is coming from Nightmesser Holdings." She shrugged and looked over at Damon as he fished the last crumbs out of his paper. "It could be a way of laundering the money from the cannabis sales."

He nodded. "Makes sense. You said you took a letter. Anything there?"

"I haven't had the chance to look yet. I left my bag in your room."

Damon squashed his empty chip paper into a ball and stood. Lucy thought she saw him grimace, but it could have been the fading light throwing shadows on his face. "Let's go take a look."

* * *

Brock Day ran the short grab of footage again. This time he let it play from beginning to end, watching the screen until Tim Hush moved out of view. He sat back in his chair and tipped his head until he was looking at the aging ceiling. Lucy Hush claimed to not recognise the guy on the street. She was either a good actress or telling the truth. His gut told him it was the latter. Yet he still had a feeling she was holding something back.

He stood up and stretched his back, listening to the base of his spine pop. He considered making another cup of coffee, but didn't think he could stomach any more of the instant muck in the station kitchen. Checking his watch, he was surprised to see it was almost six o'clock. He'd been at his desk for five hours straight. *No wonder my back's so jacked up.*

There were calls to be made, but not from the station. He slipped out the thumb-drive that contained his notes and the CCTV footage and shoved it in his pocket. Then, leaning over the desk, he erased any trace of the last few searches he'd made. When he was satisfied that everything was covered, he picked up his cup and left the office.

"Hi, boss." Liam Stokes looked up from his desk. "I thought you'd gone home."

Brock gave the young constable a stiff nod. "On my way out now."

"Right. No worries." Stokes twirled his pen and nodded to the empty desk in front of his. "Holsey's gone for the night. It's been quiet for the last hour. Should I call you if…" The young man let his words trail off and pointed to the front counter.

Brock clenched his teeth and let out a frustrated whistle. "If what?"

Stokes shifted in his seat and looked around like he was expecting help from the empty station. "I just mean… If, you know…"

"No." Brock hooked his hands on his hips, the mug dangling from his thumb. "I don't know."

"Just if things go off." Stokes' cheeks were colouring, turning the young man's face a deep shade of red. "That's all." The last words were little more than a mumble.

Brock headed for the kitchen. "Don't call me. Get hold of Holsey. He's on call tonight. It's in the roster." He tapped the sheet of paper pinned to the board on the far wall. Leaving the station in Stokes' hands was like letting a child watch a barbeque. It was all fun, games and snaggers until someone got burned.

Once he'd dumped his cup in the kitchen, Brock headed for the back door. "Night, boss," Stokes called as the door slammed closed, shutting off anything else the young man might have to say.

The small non-descript house came with the job. A short ride from the station, but enough time for Brock to replay his meeting with Lucy over again. With so much on his mind, she was one extra problem he had to square away. She knew something, but what and how much he wasn't sure. There was a moment earlier today when she'd finished watching her brother on the screen, her eyes were glassy like tears were forming and then in a blink they were gone. Brock tapped the steering wheel and pulled into the tiny driveway at the front to his house. Like most reporters, she was good at keeping her emotions in check, but he was sure she wanted to tell him something.

He climbed out of the car and let himself in the front door. It was almost fully dark now and the house was silent. Brock stood in the narrow hall and listened, making sure there was no one waiting in the shadows. It was a precaution that bordered on paranoia, but he'd learned that sometimes paranoia was a good thing. Once certain that he was alone, he turned on the lights and entered the sitting room.

There was a nest of large white candles on the side table, decorative things that smelled like caramel. He lifted the one in the centre off its china base and took the cheap mobile phone from its hiding place. There were only two numbers programmed into the phone. Each had an identifying symbol, but no name. Brock clicked on the first number and waited.

When the call connected he didn't waste time identifying himself. "That reporter worries me. She knows something." He listened for a moment as the person on the other end spoke, then nodded to the empty room. "We might have to speed things up at this end."

A minute later he ended the call and placed the phone back under the candle. Lucy Hush was an unforeseen problem. One he suspected wasn't going away any time soon.

Without thinking he let his fingers touch the scar on his arm, rubbing at the jagged line like it was itching. He was tired. Tired of the dirty job he did. Tired of keeping up a front. He slumped onto the couch and kicked off his shoes. When all this was over he was calling it quits. But for now he was stuck in Night Town.

* * *

"Roberta Stemms." Lucy read the letter dated just one week earlier. "This is to Samson Nightmesser from someone called Maureen Low, the director of St Ruben's Aged Care Facility." Perched cross-legged on Damon's bed, Lucy flicked a lock of hair off her shoulder and continued to read. "So, a nursing home. Okay, they're moving Mrs Stemms to the High Care facility and want to know if Samson would like to visit." Lucy looked up at Damon and used her fingers to make air quotation marks. *"To make the transition less daunting for Mrs Stemms."*

Damon raised his eyebrows. "Hm… Does it say anything about their relationship? Is Samson her nephew?"

Lucy shook her head. "Only that a familiar voice might help elevate any anxiety Mrs Stemms might experience due to the move." She held the letter out to Damon. "Take a look. It's strange they've written to Nightmesser and not emailed him."

As Damon read the letter, Lucy found herself wondering if they were wasting their time worrying about an old lady Samson kept in a nursing home. If Nightmesser was involved in drugs and maybe even murder, what could Roberta Stemms possibly have to do with the whole thing? She wasn't sure why she even took the letter in the first place. Only that it had been a sort of spur of the moment thing, probably because she was so freaked out in Samson's creepy house.

Damon had pulled the chair away from the desk and turned it so he was sitting facing her. He finished reading and put the letter on the desk, but didn't speak right away. His eyes narrowed like he was thinking, straining to see something in the distance. Lucy couldn't help smiling. She could almost hear the thoughts swirling in his head.

"That field is on Nightmesser property. There's no way it could be that close to the quarry and Samson not know about it." Lucy wasn't sure where he was heading, but liked listening to him think aloud. "But Nightmesser's loaded so why would he want to get involved in drugs?" She was still trying to come up with an answer when Damon plunged ahead. "That part isn't adding up, unless..." He stopped and got up and started rifling through the folder, pulling out the collection of articles with the photos of young men.

He laid the sheets of paper on the floor, each piece a few centimetres apart. "What do you see?"

Lucy clamoured to the edge of the bed and stood over the articles, focusing on the images. Each man had a similar look, not features or colouring, but something in the pose. She was trying to put her finger on the quality that made them so alike when Damon said something that made her chest constrict.

"They look lost. You can see it in their eyes."

For a second it felt like a breath was trapped in her lungs, trying to burst free but unable to push its way past her throat. That dreamy 'checked-out' look she'd seen on Tim's face so many times, it was present in each of the young men's faces. They were all fractured in some way, just like Tim.

"So, what does it mean?" When she found her breath, the words came out in a rush. "Do you think that these men were easy to draw into something illegal because they were… damaged?" The last word tasted bitter on her tongue.

"Yes." He rubbed the back of his neck. "No. I'm not sure, but what if Nightmesser isn't in this for the money?"

It took her a few seconds to work out what Damon was trying to tell her. "You think Samson's pay-off is the young men?" The horror of the realisation made her stomach sour and the greasy fish and chips that tasted so delicious only an hour ago threatened to jump back up her throat.

She covered her mouth and swallowed hard, pushing down the shudder of nausea. If Damon was right then Tim's fate was worse than she could have imagined.

"Jesus." The word was muffled under her hand like a groan.

Damon took hold of her arm. "Are you okay?" She let him pull her to the bed. "Here. Sit down."

Grateful for something solid under her, Lucy let her head hang forward and pulled in a deep breath. Her stomach lurched a second time, but not with the same force and suddenness. She heard Damon running water in the bathroom. When she looked up he handed her a glass of water, which she took with an unsteady hand.

"I'm okay." She took a sip of water then set the glass down on the bedside table. It had happened to her before, this wave of nausea and shaking. It was a reaction to stress. Something she thought she'd put behind her a long time ago. But since the other day on the road when she hit the fox, the old familiar feeling had returned.

Damon crouched down in front of her and placed his hands on her knees. They were eye-level, as close as they'd ever been. So close she could see tiny flecks of black adding depth to his whiskey-coloured eyes. "I'm sorry." He frowned. "I was thinking aloud. I forgot how hard this must be for you." There was a gentleness in the way he spoke that she hadn't heard before. It made her want to put her head on his shoulder and tell him all the sad secrets of her life. *Oh God. I really am a mess.*

"It's okay." The sickness was passing and her limbs no longer felt like pudding. "I don't expect you to keep worrying about my feelings. Whatever has happened to Tim, I want to know." She could feel the warmth of his hands through her jeans. It felt reassuring. "I can handle it." He looked uncertain, but nodded.

"I know."

As the nausea subsided, she felt a rush of relief. Not just because she was no longer close to throwing up, but also because Damon hadn't tried to tell her she was out of her depth or that it was too dangerous. When he said he knew she could handle it, she believed him and that went a long way to alleviating her bout of anxiety.

"So, what does all this have to do with the old lady?" She wanted to push on and work out their next step. Maybe if she didn't linger on what might have happened to her brother she could fool her body into cooperating.

Damon stood and began shuffling the articles together, sweeping them off the floor and back into the file. "We have a few options." He was leaning against the desk now, the folder in his hand. "We can go to the police and let them take a look at the field behind the quarry." He tossed the file on the desk. "But in a town this small I'd be surprised if there wasn't someone covering up for the little cottage industry Nightmesser has going on the side."

"What's the other option?" Lucy asked, beginning to see where he was going.

"We do a little background digging on Samson Nightmesser. No one in town is talking." He shrugged and picked up the letter.

Lucy smiled and finished the thought for him. "So, we ask Roberta Stemms to fill in the blanks."

Chapter Eleven

With little traffic, the early morning drive to Busselton was easy, reminding Lucy of a different time in her life. Car trips with her parents and little brother. Starting early to beat the school holiday rush and stopping at windswept white beaches so Tim could collect shells, his chubby legs tottering across the sand as grumpy seagulls cawed and swooped. The memories stirred up a mixture of grief and longing. Not longing to be a child again, but the need to belong to something bigger than herself.

"Maybe we should have phoned ahead." Damon was driving, his eyes locked on the road as the slash of black led them through lush countryside.

Lucy stretched. Still only partly awake, she lifted the coffee from the cup holder and took a sip. The liquid was tepid and nearing the dregs, but it was strong and rich, helping to chase the fluff away and let her mind regain something close to alertness. "I've always had more success with surprise visits. Don't worry. I'm a master at talking my way into places."

"I'll bet you are." He gave her a sideways glance that was almost comical in its amusement.

The night before, when Lucy was about to return to her room at the motel, there was a moment when it seemed the air between them had shifted. Damon insisted on walking her the few metres to her door. In another man the show of protectiveness would have irritated her, but with Damon it was different. His concern lacked the usual condescension, seeming to come from a generosity of spirit that couldn't be easily faked. Outside her door his eyes in the clouded moonlight looked more like warm toffee than whiskey. There were a few seconds when neither spoke, and as the moment stretched Lucy felt the need to fill the silence.

"All right. Well, see you in the morning." She laughed, an awkward sound considering there was nothing funny. "So, set your alarm. We don't want to sleep in." Remembering the way she'd babbled made her wince with embarrassment.

She wanted him to kiss her. She wanted to kiss him, but she had little experience to speak of. So instead she'd prattled on about setting the alarm on her phone until Damon leaned in and planted a kiss on her forehead.

"Night, Lucy." He let his fingers brush her hand and then he waited while she unlocked her door and slipped inside.

Now in the car, the easy companionship of the past few days returned, making her doubt what she'd thought she'd felt the night before. And what difference did it make? They would go their separate ways in a few days and that would be the end of it. Anything more would be too complicated, especially under the circumstances.

"So, I'll drive to my mate's house and pick up my car then you go on to the nursing home and I'll meet you there."

"Yep." She checked the time on the dashboard display: almost eight-forty. The traffic would thicken when they approached Busselton, but by the time they entered the more populated area, the rush to school and work would have ebbed. With the detour to pick up Damon's car she would probably make it to St Ruben's before ten o'clock.

"We came to Busselton a few times when I was a kid." She let her head rest against the back of the seat. "Tim was only about five or six. He loved the beach." Watching the forest slip into open fields and rural properties made her think of her brother's love for the outdoors. "We were happy. Not TV family happy. We had our ups and downs, but…" She rubbed her palms together between her legs, not really sure why she was talking about her childhood. Since her brother went missing, the emotions had become like bubbles in a murky pond. After years of being compressed below the surface, they were floating to the top, bursting through with memories. Painful memories disguised as fond recollections.

"Do your parents know Tim's missing?" Damon's voice was soft, suggesting he sensed this was tender ground.

Lucy spotted a home set back from the road, a sort of modern farm house at the end of a long track. In the crisp morning light the outline of the roof against the firmament reminded her of a child's drawing: smoke rising from a chimney drifting upwards on a glacial blue sky.

"Our parents are…" Even after so many years she had difficulty saying it aloud. "They're both dead."

"I'm sorry." He pulled in a breath. "So, you're doing all this alone?"

She kept her eyes on the house, not wanting to look at him while she spoke. "Yes. It's just me and Tim. When our parents died he was only fifteen, so I'm used to looking after him." She turned her head to watch the idyllic house disappearing behind them.

"So, who looks after you?" It wasn't what she'd expected him to say. Most people asked for details or said something pedestrian. Damon's question startled her and, for a moment, she couldn't answer.

114

What was the answer? *I have no one.* Family friends and a few cousins in Victoria. A large gathering at the double funeral. Her parents' friends and colleagues. She could almost see the crowd filling the small chapel. Tim in a suit he'd worn to her uni graduation, his face young and so pale he seemed to be disappearing into his grief. But when the formalities were over it was just her and Tim in the family home. A house that became silent overnight.

"I was twenty-one." She folded her hands together and clamped them between her knees. "I grew up fast and learned to take care of myself." She hesitated, not sure if she should go on, worried that if she told him everything, the spark of admiration she'd seen on his face when she told him about her run-in with Holsey would dissolve into pity.

She almost changed the subject and even had a glib joke on the tip of her tongue, but Damon put his hand on her arm and something in her gave. It wasn't a break, more of a release. For the first time in twelve years she wanted to tell someone what happened.

"I'd just graduated with a degree in journalism. I remember wondering if I was ready to be a grown-up, because I had an internship lined up in Victoria and it would be my first real experience away from home." As she started talking, the images came like a rapid-fire slideshow. The dinner at the Barbican, drinking champagne and laughing through tears as her dad welled up wishing her a happy twenty-first. *You're meant for great things, sweetheart.* His voice full of pride and a little sadness.

"It was the big surprise of the evening." Her throat was tight, but there were no tears in her eyes. "When we left the restaurant, my parents had the valet bring around the car they'd bought me for my birthday." She couldn't help smiling at the memory. "A Golf, bright yellow. God, I was so happy. So surprised and happy. It was like my life was just beginning."

Damon was silent, listening, his hand still on her arm. There was more traffic now, not thick but constant. "Tim wanted to drive home with me in the new car, but Mum told him I wanted to have the first drive alone so I could enjoy my present." She turned to look at Damon. He had one hand draped on the wheel in a casual pose, but his eyes, when they met hers were sombre, little lines creasing the skin at the corners. "She was sensitive, always sort of knowing what people needed. I guess Tim's like her in that way."

Like she was getting ready to plunge into freezing water, she took a deep breath before continuing. "I drove home in my new car and Mum and Dad followed with Tim. I was so focused on checking out the cool features, I must have lost them on the way. It was only when I reached home and they weren't behind me I even noticed they were gone."

The words were tumbling out now. Lucy was barely aware that she was speaking. At some point Damon pulled off the road and parked the Saab in a rest area. It was like being back there, standing on the driveway next to her little yellow car, watching each set of headlights, expecting her family to pull up, and her phone ringing. The noise muddled up in her mind and blended with the strangled cries coming out of her mouth as the police officer told her there'd been an accident.

In the confines of the Saab, she could almost feel the tingle of antiseptic and bleach on the insides of her nostrils. Lucy couldn't remember if it was a doctor or a nurse at the hospital leading her to a private room. The woman's mouth moving and the words not making sense. How could her father be gone?

She shook her head and blinked, only now really taking in her surroundings. They were parked beside a sign detailing tourist attractions in the south west. Lowering her window, she took a long breath, letting the cold air flush away the phantom smell that was coating the back of her throat.

"Are you okay?" Damon removed his seat belt and turned so he was facing her.

Lucy nodded, but the movement was more of a wobble. "Yeah. It's just... vivid, you know?"

"Come on." Damon opened the door. "I need to stretch my legs."

They walked along the trail to the rest area, which was more of a patch of flattened yellow grass with a few log seats. Behind them was the hiss of tyres along the highway and the rumble of engines. Damon swiped at one of the logs then sat so Lucy took her place beside him.

"My father died in the accident. On impact, they said." Lucy puffed out a dry laugh. "Drunk driver. A teenage girl going the wrong way on the freeway." She heard Damon make a clicking sound with his tongue. "We turned my mum's life support off three days later. Tim was in an induced coma. When he regained consciousness, I had to tell him they were both gone."

"Jesus, Lucy." Damon's voice was husky. "That's why you knew he wouldn't miss your birthday."

"Yes. After the accident, he changed. It was like I'd lost the three of them really. He was never sullen or angry, just... checked-out. I don't know if it was the head injury or grief." She shrugged. "Maybe a combination, but something in him died and he couldn't settle. Not with his friends. Not in school, so he dropped out and tried to find a job, but he just kept sinking deeper into depression. There was a stint in Graylands, a psychiatric hospital. Then he started disappearing, sleeping rough, but he always found his way back for my birthday."

She turned on the log seat so her face was towards the road and let the wind blow back her hair. This was the most she'd ever talked about the accident with anyone, even Tim. And as painful as it was there was also some relief.

"These memories..." She closed her eyes. "I'm fine most of the time, but then they come from nowhere." She opened her lids and waved her hand in the air. "It's like something stirs them up and I'm back there. I can't remember the good times anymore without the dark images riding their tail."

Damon's dark hair lifted on the breeze and she was suddenly struck by how tired he looked. "Some memories are so clear," he said. "It's like falling back into them. They have a life of their own." He rubbed the back of his neck. "They're always playing out – waiting for you, wanting to pull you in so you can play your part over and over again."

He spoke with a weariness that pulled at her heart. A weariness she recognised as personal experience. He stood and brushed off the back of his pants. "We'd better get going." He held his hand out to her.

She hesitated. "How do you stop yourself from falling back in?" She tried to make her voice light, but she could hear the longing in her question.

"You find something to hold on to," he said.

* * *

St Ruben's Aged Care Facility sat within crowded gardens. It was a sprawling Seventies-style building with Spanish inspired arches and raw brick walls. Lucy parked to the right of the building in an area marked for visitors. The emotions that had welled up on the drive to Busselton were still raw, but there was also a lightness that came from letting go and sharing the past. That feeling left Lucy slightly drained, but ready to tackle the job ahead of her.

Before entering the main doors, she removed her coat and draped it over her arm. She rolled her shoulder and put everything but the task ahead of her at the back of her thoughts. She had a part to play and her brother's life might depend on how well she performed.

The inside of St Ruben's was clean and welcoming, if a little outdated. The front desk was tucked to the left, a subtle but unmistakable reminder that this was an institution and not a spacious home.

"Good morning." The receptionist, a plump young woman with tight cork-screw curls, gave Lucy a kind smile paired with raised eyebrows.

"Hi." Lucy approached the desk, noticing the odour of pine air freshener. Experience had taught her that it was always best to keep things simple and only offer as much information as necessary. "I'm here to see Mrs Stemms."

"Yes, of course." The woman hesitated, the smile still firmly in place. "Are you…?"

Lucy knew where this was going, but didn't give anything up. "Yes, I'm a visitor."

It wasn't what the young receptionist was hoping for, but Lucy gave the girl props for not missing a beat. "That's fine." She gestured to a set of chairs near the door. "Please take a seat and I'll call through to let them know you're here."

Lucy made herself comfortable, picking up a month-old magazine and pretending to flick through the pages as she strained to listen to the hushed call. At one point she caught the name Maureen. Lucy wasn't surprised that unknown visitors were referred to the director. She once worked on a story where an elderly man in a nursing home started receiving visits from a distant cousin. Over the course of six months, the cousin managed to get the old man to sign a new will and give out his bank details, as well as handing over a very valuable ring that belonged to the old guy's late wife. Places like St Ruben's were responsible for caring for very vulnerable people. It was nice to see them taking some precautions on who they let in.

In the few moments Lucy had before the director arrived, she scanned the reception area and what she could see of the sitting room. The facility was well maintained and kitted out with comfortable furnishings. If she had to guess, Lucy would say St Ruben's was a high-end facility: all bright curtains and large sunny windows. Nothing like the grim industrial home Lucy visited when putting the story on the old man together.

Maureen Low entered through the sitting room, her beige heels clacking on the hardwood floor. Lucy was the only person in the waiting area, so the director approached her with a welcoming smile and an outstretched hand.

"Hello. I'm Maureen. I'm the director of St Ruben's." Lucy shook the woman's hand and was about to stand when the director sat in the other chair. "Denise tells me you've asked to see Mrs Stemms."

Above the smile, Maureen Low's erudite brown eyes were watchful. "Yes. That's right." Lucy hoped her face looked open and guileless, but she could see the director was waiting for more. "Mr Nightmesser asked me to visit on his behalf. I'm his secretary." As a journalist, Lucy wouldn't have dreamed of posing as someone else to get information. But she wasn't trying to get a story. Nor did she have time to worry about the ethical implications of what she was doing. This was for her brother. "Mr Nightmesser wanted me to offer his apologies for not coming himself, but..." Lucy spread her hands wide. "He has so many business and charitable commitments." The carefully rehearsed story rolled off her tongue with ease. *Jesus, I'm a good liar.*

There was a moment, just a second or so, when Maureen seemed to be thinking, but then her smile widened and Lucy's heart skipped a beat. "Of course. I understand. Although..." Lucy waited, her heart jumping into a gallop. The sound was so loud in her ears she worried the director would hear the thudding. "I was a little surprised that Mr Nightmesser didn't answer any of my emails." The woman frowned. "Sending the letter was a bit of last resort really, but poor Mrs Stemms' eyesight has deteriorated and she does get quite emotional. I was hoping your employer might come and chat to her about the move."

Lucy nodded. Looking sympathetic wasn't difficult. She could only imagine what it must be like to lose the ability to see and cope with the world around you. The idea of being so helpless almost made her shiver. "Yes. It's a good thing I check Mr Nightmesser's mail." It wasn't really a lie. She had looked through the man's letters. "I'm afraid he's not very good at checking his emails."

"Hm." The director brushed at her lap, seeming to swipe at an invisible stain. "Well, it's nice he sent you." She seemed to want to say more but changed her mind. "Mrs Stemms is in the garden. I'll take you through." And just like that Lucy was in.

The garden at the rear of St Ruben's was similar to the one in the front, overcrowded with rose bushes and bougainvillea. The roses sat in endless rows, their branches – bare of life in the winter chill – reminded Lucy of bent fingers rising from the earth. In contrast, the bougainvillea, lush and waxy, hung in pots and scrambled over walls, spreading its thorny branches wherever it found purchase. The overall effect was rather chaotic and overpowering. Lucy followed Maureen along a paved area leading to a cluster of peppermint trees where a woman wearing dark wraparound glasses sat in a wheelchair.

As they approached, Maureen spoke in a whisper. "Mrs Stemms can get confused, so don't be surprised if she seems a little muddled. Anything you can pass on from Mr Nightmesser, a message or news on Night Town will make her happy." Lucy nodded as Maureen continued, "She talks about her time with the Nightmesser family almost constantly. So, if you let her know that Mr Nightmesser wants her to make the move to a new room, it might help." Lucy couldn't help being touched by the director's concern. She wondered what Maureen would say if she knew the real reason for the visit.

They stopped a few metres away. "Mrs Stemms?" Maureen's voice was gentle and cheerful. The old woman's head was bent low like she'd nodded off. "Mrs Stemms?"

The director pitched her voice a little higher and the woman in the wheelchair looked up, her chin pointed in the opposite direction.

"Mrs Stemms, it's Maureen." The woman's head turned in their direction.

"Maureen?" Roberta Stemms' voice was rich and accented. "Is that you, love?"

"Yes." Maureen moved closer. "I have a visitor for you. A young lady sent by Mr Nightmesser. She wants to have a chat with you." The director turned to Lucy and nodded for her to approach. "She's his secretary."

Mrs Stemms touched the side of her glasses. "Nathan doesn't have a secretary."

Lucy's stomach flipped uncomfortably. She'd come all this way only to be caught in a lie. Her arms broke out in a warm sweat as she clutched her coat, waiting for the director to turn to her with an accusing stare. Her mind scrabbled, trying to formulate an answer.

"No, dear." Maureen spoke slowly. "She's Samson's secretary."

Lucy realised the old lady thought they were talking about Samson's father and her stomach relaxed. Mrs Stemms clasped her large hands together like she was about to start clapping. "Sammy sent her?"

"Yes, that's right." Lucy spoke up. "He wanted me to come and give you his regards."

The old lady's face broke into a smile, exposing teeth too regular and white to be real. "Oh, I thought he'd forgotten me."

Maureen moved around the back of Mrs Stemms' chair and nodded for Lucy to follow. She clasped the handles and began pushing the old lady towards a wrought iron table and chairs set under a wide frame draped in more climbing plants. "I'll just set you up here so you and Lucy can have a nice visit."

The old lady's chin bobbed as the director wheeled her to the sitting area. "Who's Lucy?"

"I'm Samson's secretary. My name's Lucy." She sat down opposite the old lady, wondering if this was all a huge waste of time. Mrs Stemms was obviously very confused. Lucy doubted she could tell her anything useful.

"I'll leave you to it then." Maureen checked her watch. "Someone will be out to collect Mrs Stemms in about twenty minutes so she can have her medication and use the bathroom before lunch. If you need anything," she pointed to the path, "just go back in the way we came and ask Denise." Before heading back down the pathway, the director paused and touched the old lady's shoulder. "Enjoy your visit, dear." Mrs Stemms reached up and patted Maureen's hand. There was something motherly in the way the old lady touched the director that made Lucy's heart lurch with loneliness.

As Maureen's heels clacked back towards the building, Lucy turned her attention on Mrs Stemms. She wore a fluffy pink cardigan, hand knitted and chunky, the colour a stark contrast to the old lady's pale cheeks.

"It's nice to meet you, Mrs Stemms." Lucy dumped her coat on the circular iron table along with her handbag. Normally, she'd be taking notes, but as Samson's secretary it would look strange.

"Call me Roberta." The old lady was looking in Lucy's direction, but the angle was off, her gaze staring past Lucy's shoulder. "How is Sammy?"

"He's very well. Busy with a fundraiser to build a new community centre in Night Town." Lucy kept as close to the truth as possible, knowing it would be safer and less likely to trip her up.

Roberta chuckled a warm sound. "Wonders never cease. But if the lad's developed a generous streak, I'm happy."

Lucy frowned. "He wasn't so generous when you knew him?" Lucy still didn't know Samson's connection to the old lady, but couldn't come right out and ask.

"Sure, I can't blame him for keeping things to himself. He's had a difficult life." She pulled the cardigan together and began fiddling with the buttons. "A sad beginning for that child."

Lucy stood. "Let me help you with the buttons."

"You're a kind girl. I can see why Sammy hired you."

Lucy leaned over Roberta, noticing the scent of baby powder and shampoo. "You've known him a long time."

"Sure. I worked in that house since before he was born." She nodded as Lucy slipped the last button in place. "Helped his poor mother through her pregnancy. I was hired as a housekeeper, but I could see the girl was struggling. Lidia was such a sweet thing. It would have been unchristian of me to not do what I could." She patted Lucy's hand. "Thank you, love."

Her hand lingered on the old lady's shoulder. There was something calming about chatting with Roberta. Lucy never knew her grandmothers. Both had died before she was born. She couldn't help wondering if this would have been what it was like to have a nana. She felt a stab of guilt. Lying to the woman was harder than she thought it was going to be.

"What was I saying?" Roberta looked up as Lucy crossed back to the chair.

"You were telling me about Samson's mother."

"Oh yes. What a tragic waste. And so young." Roberta was shaking her head. Thin streaks of red buried amongst the mostly silver hair caught the sunlight. At the mention of a tragedy Lucy's ears pricked up. She wanted to push, but knew it was better to stay silent and wait. "It was the shock. That poor baby."

Lucy was having trouble following the old lady's fractured thoughts, but she guessed it was something about Samson's sister. She remembered him mentioning a birth defect.

"After Lidia took her life, well, Nathan… I mean, Mr Nightmesser went to pieces. Blamed that poor baby."

Roberta pulled a tissue out of her sleeve and lifted the dark glasses so she could dab her eyes.

When she looked up, Lucy bit back a gasp. The woman's eyes were covered in a milky film unlike anything Lucy had ever seen. A thick layer, like the skin on a white pudding, covered not only the irises and pupils, but the entire eye.

"He was a good man. I won't have anyone saying otherwise." Lucy was relieved when Roberta lowered her glasses and the old lady's strange eyes were no longer visible.

"Yes," Lucy managed. "I'm sure he was." A pair of wattle birds landed on the bougainvillea-draped frame above Roberta's head. The creatures regarded the two women with black, shiny eyes. Samson Nightmesser and his sister obviously had had quite a sad childhood, but she couldn't see how anything the woman had said so far would help them find Tim.

"Sure, none of it was the child's fault," Roberta continued. "The baby came into the world as God made him." A door opened in the distance and Lucy could hear someone approaching.

"Him?" Lucy couldn't help interrupting. Either the old lady was more confused than she realised or something was very off. "I thought you were talking about Samson's sister, Samantha."

Roberta shook her head. "No." She drew the word out. "Samson doesn't have a sister." She pushed the tissue back up her sleeve. "That boy and the stories he'd tell. It got so I didn't like my little boy hanging around the house. It wasn't right for my son to be with such a mixed up young lad. Don't get me wrong. I have kind feelings for that boy, but Samson was never quite right." Her frail shoulders jerked. "Is it any wonder?"

Lucy glanced over her shoulder, spotting the nurse approaching. She was running out of time and her gut told her there was something important in what Roberta was telling her.

"So, it was Samson with the birth defect?" It wasn't the sort of question Nightmesser's secretary should be asking, but Roberta seemed too enveloped in reminiscing to notice.

"Birth defect?" Roberta's creased brow furrowed until her forehead was a nest of V-shaped lines. "You could call it that. To be a mix of both sexes." She made a clicking sound with her tongue. "I think it was more of a curse."

Lucy was at a loss for words, her mind trying to process what the old woman had said. If Roberta was right, *of course she's right, why wouldn't she be?* Then that changed everything *and* nothing.

"Mrs Stemms." The nurse, a dark-skinned woman in a navy-blue smock, stepped up to the wheelchair. "Time for the bathroom?"

Lucy was still grappling with how the shocking information on Samson might impact all those young men's disappearances. "Wait." It came out too loud. Both Roberta and the nurse turned to stare at Lucy. "I mean… I just wanted to ask Roberta something."

"What is it, love?" Roberta's head was starting to droop back down to her chest. Her voice was suddenly thick with fatigue.

"Sorry, dear." The nurse was already kicking the brakes free on the old lady's chair. "Mrs Stemms needs the toilet and her medication."

"Okay. Yes, sorry." Lucy followed as the woman pushed Roberta onto the path. She couldn't just leave it like this, not when there were so many unanswered questions. "Can I telephone you, Roberta? Just to chat some more?"

"Sure, I'd love another chat. Bye, love." The wheels on the chair pinged as the nurse headed back towards the building.

Chapter Twelve

The lights never came on when Samantha entered. Tim knew she was hiding something from him, but wished he could see her face. Any face that could wipe away the memory of the rubber mask. Just to see another human mouth and nose, the features set in warmth or anger. As long as they were real – *human*.

When the door creaked open he didn't try to sit up and watch her feet – this time clad in suede pumps – clack into the room. The lantern was by her side as usual. He could make out the sound of a paper bag rustling and see the big low pocket on her full skirt.

"I've brought you something to eat." She settled herself on the small bench just out of reach. "Cheese and tomato." She giggled, an unpleasant sound that reminded Tim of the cries he'd hear in the night during his time in the hospital.

He didn't answer. The cut on his lip, like a worn-out zip, threatened to open at the slightest movement. She placed the lantern on the stone floor and slid the bag in his direction. As he moved forward to take the food, Samantha gasped.

"Oh, Tim. Your poor face." There was surprise in her voice but no real sympathy. "The bruises, they're so…" she was breathing heavily, "…so vivid."

He pulled the sandwich out of the bag and broke off a hunk of bread. In spite of his injuries, his stomach howled with anticipation.

"I've been working on a new piece." She crossed her legs, nylon stockings swishing together. "I wish you could see it. It's very raw and expressive." The giggle again. "I suppose that sounds like I'm blowing my own trumpet."

Tim pushed another piece of bread into his mouth, forcing himself to chew slowly so as not to aggravate his lip. Her visits were the only real human contact he'd had since being brought to the cell. Until now he had felt a sort of Stockholm-like affection for the woman. But with the last beating something inside him changed. Or maybe grew. He wasn't sure.

"You're very quiet today." She leaned forward slightly, the lantern revealing blonde tresses. "Is there something wrong?"

Laughter built in his throat, bitter and angry, but he shoved a clump of sandwich in his mouth and muffled the sound. He was glad she kept herself out of reach, because the urge to leap across the room and grab her by the throat was almost overwhelming.

Until his latest visit from the masked man, he'd felt pity for Samantha. Frustrated with her unwillingness to help him, but sorry nonetheless. Now that had all changed. He realised she was guilty. As guilty as her brother. Only somehow Samantha was worse because she spoke to him like a friend.

"Tim?" She was waiting for him to speak. "Have I upset you?"

He promised himself he wouldn't speak, wouldn't play his part as her sad friend, but the words couldn't be stopped. "Upset me?"

She was nodding. He could see the tips of her hair moving in the light. "Look at me." He crawled forward so his face was in the lantern's arc. "Can you see?" His voice was a shriek, barely recognisable as his own. "If you don't know why I'm upset, then you're as twisted as your brother."

"Oh." The sound was one of shock. "I... I didn't—"

"I'm going to die here." His voice had lost its indignation. "He'll kill me next time or the time after that. And you..." He lifted his manacled foot and the chains clanked like something out of an old horror movie. Tim shuffled his butt forward and pointed at her. "You just let it happen." Her feet were shifting now like she was getting ready to run. "Just go away and leave me alone." He thought he had no tears left, but he was wrong.

"Please, Tim, let me—"

"You're..." He tried to think of something cruel to say, something that would send her running from the room. He was risking everything. The food and water she brought him. Any chance of convincing her to let him go. "You're a freak."

Once the words were out he felt a flicker of regret, but refused to let himself take them back. She made a sound, a strangled cry, and jumped to her feet. It was the chance he'd hoped for. With him halfway off the sleeping bag and near the light, all it took was for Samantha to step a little too far in his direction.

When he pounced it was with speed he wasn't sure he could muster. He clamped his hands around her waist and pulled her towards him, feeling the hard body beneath the soft cotton blouse. She was screaming, a croaky old-lady scream, loud enough to bounce off the stone walls and hurt his ears. In the struggle he stupidly thought about his ears being as unused to noise as his eyes were to light.

She fought like a wild animal, writhing with more strength than he'd bargained for. The cell filled with heavy breathing and grunts as the two of them struggled. Tim tried to get a grip on her upper body but Samantha landed an elbow to his already bruised and battered ribs. Tim heard something snap. The noise was like a bunch of dry pasta cracked over a pot of water. A pain, unlike any he'd experienced so far, stabbed at him from inside and the strength in his arms began to fizzle out.

As Samantha wrenched herself free, he made one last grab and tore her skirt. She howled like a wounded pig and scampered out of the cell, slamming the heavy door with a splintering *whomp*.

Tim rolled left, his arms wrapped around his rib cage. Something moved under his skin with a sickening creak. He blew out an agonised breath as spittle, bitter like copper and salt, sprayed his chin.

His rib was broken. At least one, maybe more, but he had the lantern and whatever the bulky object was he'd ripped from her pocket.

Each breath was hot agony, pierced by razor sharp jabs. Curled on his side, Tim focused on slowing his breath. When the exhaustion of the struggle subsided, he managed to control his breathing into shallow swallows, minimising the torture.

With his heart pounding he pulled himself into a sitting position, left arm clamped to his ribs like he was holding them together. His eyes fell on the lantern and in spite of the pain, he laughed.

"Ow." Tim regretted the moment of celebration as his broken rib stabbed somewhere deep and fleshy. "Careful. Careful," he whispered around a bloody grin and scooted forward until his manacled left foot was stretched out behind him.

Tim hooked the rigid plastic handle with his index finger and dragged the lantern closer. For one terrifying second the light almost slipped from his grasp and his heart jack-hammered in his chest. He hissed out a breath and snatched the handle with a shaking hand, clasping it close, the glow lighting up his torn and filthy shirt.

He had it. He had light. After what felt like weeks, he was no longer in the dark. With the new ability to see his surroundings came a sort of elation that made him want to cheer. It had been a long time since anything brought him that level of happiness in or outside the cell. The burst of joy made him think of Lucy. She would be looking for him. Lucy would never give up. If not for himself then for her, he had to try. He wouldn't sentence her to a lifetime of searching and misery, not when she'd been through so much.

There was no time to waste celebrating, not when Samantha was probably telling her brother about the attack. The masked man could appear at any time and right now Tim was in no condition to put up anything close to a fight.

"Not yet." Tim uncurled his left arm and opened his hand.

From her pocket, he'd taken a small tool that resembled a mini trowel; he'd gripped it so tightly that it had left an imprint in his palm. The red wooden handle was cracked and faded from years of use. Smudged with dry paint, the stainless-steel trowel end was small, almost heart-shaped and flexible. Tim had been required to participate in art classes during his time in treatment. He recognised the tool as a palette scraper.

"Thank you, Samantha." He swiped at his chin, barely noticing the blood on the back of his hand.

The plan to attack the woman had been brewing since his last beating. Only as the idea formed he'd had little hope of doing more than securing the lantern. *Or wrap the chain around her neck and wait for the brother.* But when he saw her bulging pocket, Tim knew he had to try for whatever she was carrying. A small part of his mind wanted to believe it was a mobile phone, but he told himself any variation on a tool would do. *I'm becoming a real optimist.* In the end he was relieved he hadn't hurt Samantha. He had the tool and the light and a broken rib or two. What good would it do to injure the woman?

Somewhere in the building the dripping tap continued its endless rhythm as Tim went to work on the tool. The constant cold in the cell made his fingers numb and clumsy. It took him a few minutes of rocking the metal like a loose tooth to remove the stainless-steel arm from the red handle. Once the palette scraper was in two pieces he pressed the thin prong that had previously been embedded in the handle against the stone floor. By keeping the narrow bar of metal at a ninety degree angle, Tim was able to use the handle to press the flexible stainless steel tine into an L shape.

Creating the small L-bar took no longer than five minutes, but by the time he held the tool to the light, his bruised face was shiny with sweat. "It'll work." He rubbed his arm over his forehead and cheeks. "It will."

Samantha's brother always turned the light on before entering. But that didn't mean he wouldn't enter in the dark. The guy was a lunatic. Tim shuffled back a few centimetres so the chain had some slack. The man in the mask wasn't just crazy, he was a sadist. A violent sadist who enjoyed beating someone helpless. Tim stopped moving and cocked his head, sure he'd heard movement beyond the door. Just thinking about the man made Tim's skin cold with fear. The guy terrified him and not just because of the violence. The cold eyes peering through the holes in the rubber mask were so devoid of emotion it was like staring into a grey swamp. A place where light and hope never shone.

Tim couldn't shake the feeling that his captor was close by. Maybe he was always close. He pulled the lantern alongside his ankle, grateful for the circle of light in the dark cell. If he had any chance, he had to push past the fear and free himself.

Leaning forward to reach his ankle sent off a stab of pain in his chest. Tim gritted his teeth and took hold of the cuffs. His ankle was encased in fairly straightforward, ratcheted double-lock handcuffs. Not difficult to pick if you knew what you were doing. He wiped a bubble of blood from his lower lip and pushed the makeshift lock pick into the keyhole.

Reading about the handcuff mechanism and how to pick it was fine, fascinating even, but putting that knowledge into practice was something he wasn't altogether sure about. He swallowed and turned the pick counter-clockwise. The first part was the kicker, disengaging the double lock bar. This took finesse and a solid yet slim tool. His fingers were warm now. Moving with more agility, he pushed the pick against the tip of the first bar. In his mind Tim could visualise the mechanism with perfect clarity, but acting through the small end of a palette scraper on the unseen component was like trying to thread a needle in the dark.

With the pick pressing on the double lock bar, Tim slowly applied pressure. Droplets of perspiration were clinging to the tips of his hair. Despite the chilled air in the cell, his body was feverish from the small exertions. The smell of the long-drop toilet seemed to be intensifying, working its way past his tonsils and clogging his throat. He pushed the pick another fraction, praying the metal wouldn't bend and give under the pressure. In response, the lock bar shifted.

He wanted to whoop with relief, but kept his concentration on the tool. All that was left now was a clockwise turn to push the first lock bar down, giving the ratchet teeth room to move. Tim's fingers were slippery and his grip on the pick started to falter. He spun the tool right and clicked the second lock bar down. Without pausing Tim used his left hand to pull the ratchet arm free and allow the cuff to open.

He pulled the cuff off his ankle and let his head tilt back so the tears in his eyes dripped over his temples. When he looked back down he almost expected to see the cuff still locked around his lower leg like freeing himself had been nothing more than a heart-pounding daydream. But sure enough, his ankle, ringed with frayed skin and blood, was finally free of the restraint.

For some crazy reason an old half-forgotten nursery rhyme jumped into his thoughts. *Pop goes the weasel.* The idea made him laugh out loud, his voice deep and echoing in the silence. Tim stood, enjoying the weightless feeling in his left leg and then wincing at the stab in his side.

He pulled off his torn shirt and wrapped it around his rib cage, gasping as the fabric tightened against his broken bones. Then tying the shirt in front, he let out a shallow breath. The pressure eased the pain, not much but enough to let him move without feeling waves of blackness threatening to sweep him into unconsciousness.

"Not now." He spoke to the empty cell. "Too much to do."

* * *

Damon was waiting in the visitors' parking lot, leaning against a battered-looking Jeep with his arms folded. He appeared to be studying the gathering clouds. Seeing him there waiting for her made Lucy's already racing pulse kick up another notch.

Noticing her approach, he pushed off the car. "Anything?"

Lucy nodded and pulled her keys out of her bag. "I need to talk to you, but not here." She unlocked the Saab and pulled the driver's door open. "I noticed a pub a few streets that way." She jerked her chin to the left. "I need a drink."

"I'll follow you." Damon was already climbing into the Jeep as he spoke.

With so much to think about, Lucy was surprised that it was Damon who occupied her mind in that moment. As she pulled out of the parking lot she couldn't help admiring the man. Most people would have wanted immediate information, but Damon seemed to possess an innate sense, always knowing when actions were more important than words.

The pub she'd spotted was an old-fashioned sort of place with dark walls and a long, polished wood bar. They sat in the main bar, Lucy with a glass of house white and Damon nursing a middy. The air was thick with the heavy odour of malt and citrus, a combination that reminded her of pub food and late nights.

"It's got to mean something, doesn't it?" She'd just finished recounting her conversation, including the astonishing truth about Samson and his *sister*. "I mean he's obviously involved in the drug thing and now this." She took a swallow of wine, relishing the sharp aftertaste.

Damon had barely touched his drink. He didn't strike her as someone easily shocked, but she could see he was wrestling with this new piece of information. He sat on a padded stool, fist pressed to his chin. She waited, giving him time to think.

When he finally spoke, he seemed to be thinking aloud. "His father raised him as a boy. We know this because of his name and the newspaper article referred to Nathan being survived by his son, Samson." Damon's eyes were fixed on something behind her on the wall. "If he identifies as female, the strain of living life as a male would have been tremendous, maybe more than he could stand. He told you he had a sister named Samantha, an artist. A big departure from Samson the businessman." He frowned. "So, he sees himself as two distinct personalities: Samson and Samantha." Damon rubbed the back of his neck. "Roberta worked at the house for years yet she'd never heard of Samantha."

Lucy had an inkling where Damon was going. She put down her glass and waited.

"Could it be," Damon turned his gaze on her, "that the split in personalities is a recent thing?"

"Or," Lucy added. "Something he kept hidden while his father was alive. Roberta did say Samson was a child that told stories. Maybe the birth defect combined with the guilt his father heaped on him over the mother's suicide was all too much for Little Samson." Lucy grimaced. "It would have been unbearable for him in that house. Living a lie and believing he'd caused his own mother's death." Despite everything that he might have done, Lucy couldn't help feeling a pang of sorrow for the little boy that Nightmesser had once been. Trapped by guilt *and* his own body.

"So, something changes and Samson Nightmesser begins living a double life. Is it that much of a jump to believe he also started killing young men? Dissociative identity disorder or DID doesn't automatically make you a killer. But…" Damon drew out the last word, "from what I've read, DID is usually associated with other mental disorders such as bipolar and borderline personality disorder. Untreated, the combination could lead to a great deal of mental instability."

"Hang on." Lucy held up her hand. "How do you even know all this stuff?"

Damon took a sip of beer. "I studied psychology for a year and half before deciding it wasn't for me." He shrugged. "It's interesting stuff. I still like to read psych journals from time to time."

She was impressed but as usual turned her feelings into a joke. "What exactly did you say you did in the army?" When the question was out she realised she was only half joking.

Damon chuckled. "That sounds like something a reporter would ask." He feigned surprise. "Oh, wait."

Lucy couldn't help smiling, not so much at his joke, but the skilful way he dodged the question. "Well, in your semi-professional opinion, do you think Nightmesser is at the centre of all this?"

"I'd say he's a pretty messed up guy, which makes him a good bet for the missing men."

Lucy's heart missed a beat, thumping hard then slow. "So, you think he took Tim?" She pushed on not giving him time to answer. "We should go back to Nightmesser's house. Confront him, force him to tell us where he's keeping Tim." She was already half out of her seat when Damon caught her arm.

"Hang on, Lucy. Even if Samson is responsible for the disappearances, we still don't know the whole picture." He lowered his voice. "There's some heavy stuff going on in that town. I saw one field, but there could be more. If Samson suffers with DID, I doubt he'd be able to mastermind a set up like the one I saw behind the quarry. People with untreated DID live fractured lives, memory and time loss, mood swings, you name it."

"Then let's go to the police." She was leaning forward now, her voice an urgent whisper. "We can't afford to waste time, not now that we know who took Tim."

Damon shook his head, a single unyielding movement. "And what if the cops are involved?" He didn't give her time to answer. "If Tim's alive, the first thing they'd do is get rid of him."

For the first time since meeting Damon on the road she felt a spark of annoyance. "Then what do you suggest? We just sit around and wait until Samson does whatever it is that gets a lunatic like him off? Torture? Murder? This is my brother we're talking about." She could hear the bitterness in her words but didn't care. Her brother might be alive and being kept in Nightmesser's house; anything could be happening to him. The very thought made her want to push past Damon and his cautious warnings and run to the car.

Damon's warm amber eyes seemed to lose some of their lustre, but his gaze remained fixed on hers. She'd hurt him; it was evident in the way his jaw clenched and his posture stiffened. "Lucy." His voice was gentle. "By rushing in we could make things worse for Tim."

She let her hands drop between her legs and rubbed her palms together. As much as it wasn't what she wanted to hear, she knew Damon was right. "So, what do we do now?" Her voice was still tight, but she managed to quell her impatience.

He glanced at his watch. "My mate, the one that let me leave my car at his place, he's an ex-cop. I'll go see him and find out if he can put us in touch with someone we can trust."

It wasn't immediate action, but at least they were heading in the right direction. Lucy thought about throwing back the rest of her wine, but suddenly her stomach felt like it was lined with acid. "Okay. I'll come with you."

"No." There was an edge to his voice she hadn't heard before. A steeliness that she suspected lay just beneath the casual demeanour. She wasn't sure how she felt about this side of him, but decided that right now she needed someone with a hard edge. "You go back to Night Town and see what you can find on Roberta Stemms. Also," he tapped the table, "you said your producer wanted to send a crew."

"Yes. He's red hot to get a juicy story."

Damon paused. He seemed to be thinking something through. "Tell him to have them ready to go. If we don't get anywhere with the cops by tomorrow, we'll bring in the media." He stood. "Whoever's masterminding this whole thing can't make us all disappear."

Chapter Thirteen

It was almost two p.m. when Lucy rounded the bend in the road and Night Town, the now familiar cluster of buildings and fields that sat in a semi-circle of impenetrable forest, came into view. A kingdom owned by Samson. While her first instinct was to confront Nightmesser, she knew Damon's approach was best. She just hoped she wouldn't regret taking the cautious route.

Like the first time she saw the place, Lucy felt a shiver of disquiet as she entered the town proper. The motel parking lot was empty when she pulled in, save the manager's ancient white ute. Like the main street, the cracked bitumen slab was awash in leaves and small forest debris swept up by an approaching gale from the west.

Lucy climbed out of the car, wrestling with the hem of her coat as it swirled upwards. Pulling the puffer together with one fist, she ducked her head and ran for her room, all the while turning her face away from the wind as wild strands of hair whipped her cheeks.

Once inside, the noise of the wind continued to batter the window, throwing sticks and leaves at the pane like bushland confetti. Shivering, Lucy dumped her bag on the bed and checked the thermostat. Either it was faulty or the temperature had taken a sudden drop. She turned the dial and heard the whir of warm air swishing out of the overhead vent.

There was a plastic electric kettle on top of the bar fridge along with two Pyrex brown mugs that looked like kitsch relics from a Seventies hostess trolley. What she really needed was real coffee, but for now she'd make do with a cup of instant. Sorting through the complimentary sachets in the basket next to the kettle, she found tea, coffee and sugar. *Black coffee. Great.*

Sitting at the desk with her laptop open, she took a sip of the coffee and grimaced. It was bitter and powdery, but at least it was hot. Hands still stinging with the cold, she typed a quick email to Matt, giving him a brief outline of the progress she'd made, omitting the information on Nightmesser's birth defect and asking that he have a crew standing by, but not send them until she'd liaised with the police.

Lucy tapped a finger to her lower lip. It wasn't a complete lie. Damon was sort of liaising with the cops. Besides, Matt would be pleased she was talking to the authorities, that way he couldn't be accused of doing anything unethical or illegal. Satisfied with what she'd written, she finished by promising to keep her producer updated with any new developments.

Once the email was sent she glanced up at the window. The westerly had transformed from a gust into a gale, soughing through the parking lot in a flurry of plastic shopping bags and small branches. The aging pane vibrated as though invisible hands slapped the glass.

Lucy took another sip of the bitter liquid and shuddered. Her mind went back to the conversation with Roberta. There was something nagging at the edge of her thoughts. Something that might be important, but she couldn't quite catch hold of the idea.

"Damn." She took the cup and grabbed the cigarettes from her handbag.

After tossing the rest of the coffee into the bathroom sink, Lucy lit a smoke and clamped it between her teeth as she forced open the tiny window over the toilet. A punch of cold air burst through the narrow gap, playing over her head as she sat on the edge of the lime-green tub.

She blew out a plume of smoke and watched it drift upwards then dissipate in the cold air. Damon told her to do some digging on Roberta, but all Lucy could think about was Nightmesser's house – the stark disturbing paintings he attributed to his sister and the fortress-like exterior. It was easy to believe he could be keeping someone in that gothic atrocity.

Perched on the edge of the tub, her mind kept going back to the moment Samson opened the door. Had she been within shouting distance of her brother? She closed her eyes and pictured the moment Samson invited her inside. In her mind's eye she saw the staircase and a series of closed doors. Then as she left, looking back and seeing the curtain twitch in the upstairs window.

Lucy opened her eyes and ashed the cigarette in the empty coffee mug. She'd assumed it was Samson's sister at the window, but now Lucy wondered if maybe Samson had rushed upstairs to watch as she walked away or if someone else was in the house.

She stood and ran water into the mug, not really watching what she was doing. Could it have been Tim in the upstairs window? Maybe trying to signal her but unable to call out for some reason. The mug overflowed, splashing her hand with cold water. The shock of cold water acted like a starter's gun, propelling her to action.

Leaving the mug in the sink, Lucy darted out of the bathroom and grabbed her phone from her handbag. She called Damon, watching the wind cuff the empty parking lot. After five rings it went through to voicemail.

She hesitated before speaking. "Hi, it's Lucy. I think I saw someone in the upstairs window at Samson's house yesterday." She let out a breath, not sure what to say next. "It could have been Tim. Call me back."

Tossing the phone back in her bag, Lucy slumped onto the chair in front of the desk. Every nerve in her body told her she was close to finding her brother or at least the truth about what happened to him. But with nothing to do but wait, she decided to see if she could find anything on Roberta Stemms.

But with sluggish Wi-Fi and the need for coffee – real coffee – biting at her nerves, Lucy shut the laptop and pulled a folded piece of paper from her bag. She scrawled a quick message to Damon and grabbed her coat. Before leaving the motel, she pushed the note under Damon's door.

The streets were busy, the chill wind whipping pedestrians as they hurried along the pavement with their heads bent and shoulders curled. In contrast, the café was warm and empty except for a young woman hunched over her phone as her baby dozed in an oversized buggy. Lucy ordered a coffee in a takeaway cup, but instead of rushing back to the motel, she sat at the same table she'd used a few days ago.

Her thoughts turned to an idea she'd had a few months earlier. It was more of a dream than a real plan, but in the weeks leading up to her birthday, the daydream seemed more feasible and the idea took hold. After the accident that killed her parents, she'd kept the family home so Tim wouldn't have any more upheavals in his life. At least that's what she'd told herself at the time.

But as the years passed and Tim became more and more restless and unwilling to live in their old house, Lucy continued to cling to the idea of keeping the family home going. It was only as she approached her thirty-third year that it occurred to her that she'd kept the place, not for her younger brother, but because she couldn't let go of her old life. She realised a small part of her was clinging to the safety of the house, maybe refusing to let go of the last place she'd been truly happy.

Lost in thought, Lucy picked up her coffee and took a sip, not really seeing the street beyond the window. Maybe the house, with its happy *and* tragic memories was stopping her and Tim from moving forward. From finding a new place to build a future that wasn't shadowed by the past. If she sold the house and bought a place away from the city somewhere south of Perth with acres of land, Tim would be able to roam free and still be within the safety of their own property.

She looked down at her almost empty cup. It was a nice dream, a modest house with bushland and maybe a stream. Most of her work was out of the office so she'd only have to commute to the city a few times a week. She could even start working on the novel she'd always wanted to write. But without Tim what would be the point?

Outside, a horn blared and tyres screeched. Lucy looked up and, for a moment, didn't recognise the figure on the other side of the street. It was only as the man paused at the entrance to the bank, shoulders slightly hunched as he turned to watch the same commotion that had pulled Lucy's attention away from her musings that she recognised his profile.

Samson Nightmesser dressed in a dark coat with a silky scarf bunched at his throat. Lucy didn't notice the minor traffic skirmish; her gaze was fixed on Samson. He swiped at his thinning grey hair before turning and disappearing inside the bank.

She made the decision in less than the time it took to pick up her bag and leave the café. The house was unattended. If she went now she just might have time to get inside and find her brother. *And if he comes back and finds me at the house?* Lucy pushed the question aside and got in her car.

On her way out of town she tried calling Damon again, but he still wasn't answering. She *could* wait, drive back to the motel and sit tight, but her gut told her she might not get another crack at the empty house.

"Damon, it's me." She hesitated before finishing the voice message. If she told him what she was doing he'd most likely come rushing after her. If Tim was being kept in Samson's house, Damon showing up might not be a bad thing. But if Tim wasn't there it could make things worse. Worse for Tim. She decided to split the difference and only give Damon part of the truth. "I'm going to see Nightmesser again, see what I can find out. Don't worry. I'll be careful." It wasn't the whole truth, but it might slow him down and give her time to get in and out of the house without all hell breaking loose. She tossed the phone back in her bag just as the Saab bumped over the bridge and Night Town shrank in the rear-view mirror.

* * *

Larson jerked his chin in Damon's direction, the phone clamped to his neck. "Hang on." He pulled the phone away and held it at his side.

Damon raised his brows.

"They want a number where they can contact you." Larson kept his voice low.

Damon reeled off the number and listened as Larson passed it on to the contact on the other end of the line.

"I can't wait long," Damon said as his friend disconnected the call. "The drugs aren't my priority. All I care about is finding a couple of guys that went missing in the town."

Larson nodded. "You heard me pass that on." He shrugged. "What they do with it now is anyone's guess, but they'll probably get back to you sooner than later."

Larson Granger was one of Damon's oldest friends. After the two met in basic training, Larson decided military life wasn't for him. Something Damon suspected had more to do with homesickness than any real dislike of military service. After being discharged, Larson joined the Western

144

Australian Police Force. Sixteen years later he was an ex-cop with his own security and investigation company and Damon's sometime employer.

"You think the cops have someone on the inside?" Damon asked.

They were in Larson's office, a nondescript building in an industrial section of Busselton. "Andro was pretty sketchy, but I'd say so." Larson stood and went to the filing cabinet against the wall. "If UCOs are involved, you're in dangerous territory."

Damon repeated the acronym in his mind: UCO, undercover officers.

Larson stood at the side of the cabinet and pushed, rolling the metal locker aside to reveal a wall safe.

Damon had seen the safe before and knew what his friend kept inside. "The guys at the plantation were armed, but it looked like shotguns – farm stuff mostly." He waited while Larson turned his back, his wide shoulders blocking the safe while he put in the combination.

A few seconds later Larson turned and held out a black cotton bag. "Take this. It's loaded. It can't be traced back to me, but don't get caught with it."

Damon took the bag noting the weight of the handgun as he shoved it in his jacket pocket. "No worries." He knew Larson was talking about the stiff penalties for being caught with an unlicensed and concealed firearm. In Western Australia firearms crimes came with a stiff fine and maybe even a suspended sentence.

"Thanks, mate." Damon stood to leave. "Hopefully, I won't need it."

"If you do," Larson pointed to Damon's pocket. "Ditch it afterwards."

Damon zipped up his jacket. "If your contact gets back to me, it won't come to that."

"This reporter you said you're working with, what's she like?" A hint of a smile played around his friend's tight-lipped mouth.

Damon shrugged. "She's okay. You know, smart but hurting."

"I see." Larson steepled his fingers on his chest and fixed his clear blue eyes on Damon with an unwavering stare. His closely-cropped blonde hair looked almost white under the glare of the office light. Damon imagined suspects shrivelled under that look.

Damon made a clicking sound with his tongue. "We're just helping each other."

Larson nodded. "That's what I thought."

* * *

Damon stashed the gun under the seat and pulled out his phone. He had two new voicemails, both from Lucy. He listened to the messages and cursed under his breath. He tried calling Lucy's number before tossing his phone on the passenger seat and pulling out of the small parking lot that serviced Larson's office and the dance studio next door.

It was 3:32 when he turned onto the highway and headed south. He pushed the Jeep, trying to make up some time while the main artery out of Busselton was relatively quiet. On his right, the wind off the ocean pushed with enough force to rattle the vehicle as clouds congregated over the choppy waters like bulging lungs heavy with grey smoke.

His mind kept coming back to the things Lucy told him about her parents and the way they died. She was a strong woman, yet when she talked about her family the pain was clear in every syllable. Losing her mother and father had left a terrible scar. Not a wound visible to the naked eye, but deep and painful nevertheless. Was it any wonder she would do anything to save her brother, even risking her own life? He should have seen this coming.

It had been a long time since he'd met anyone like Lucy Hush. No, he corrected himself. He hadn't let anyone get close to him like Lucy. But that wasn't right either. That first day when he found her on the road, her smoky green eyes wide and unguarded for just a second before she tried to pretend she had everything under control. That's when it happened. With one look, she got under his skin.

As the road turned inland he had the feeling the building storm was on his heels. He was supposed to be in Night Town to find Aidan, but somehow all that had become secondary to the way he felt about Lucy. Damon checked the time: 3:50. Over the last few days he found himself getting further and further away from the real reason he was here; to put right something he could never forgive himself for, but instead he was acting like a teenager.

"What the hell am I doing?" He spoke to the empty car.

We're just helping each other, that's what he had said. But when Larson asked him about Lucy it was all he could do to not grin like an idiot. This wasn't him. *She's almost ten years younger than me. And*, he reminded himself, out of his league. But when she had thrown her arms around him at the bridge he wanted to believe there was more. Maybe something real. But he was a stubborn old bastard, set in his ways, according to his ex-wife.

When all this was over they'd each go their own way and that would be it. The most he could hope for was keeping her safe and giving her back her brother. But none of that would happen if he didn't get his pile of junk Jeep to Night Town before something happened to her.

Damon pushed the accelerator, forcing the Jeep to go beyond the speed limit. From what he'd heard about Samson Nightmesser, Lucy was putting herself in real danger going back into that house. He just hoped he wasn't too late.

Chapter Fourteen

It was too risky to leave the car outside Samson's house. If he did return before she'd had a chance to look around, the Saab would be a dead giveaway. *Dead.* Used so glibly, the word now made her cringe. At the end of the cul-de-sac and to the right was a small clearing in the dense bush. Lucy nosed the car over the concrete curb and crawled forward, grimacing as the wheels spun then took hold on the uneven ground.

She inched her way through the bush as branches screeched along the side of the vehicle. Checking the rear-view mirror, she was satisfied that the car was well clear of the road. *How the hell am I going to get back out?* She turned off the engine and tried to open the door. Something was blocking it, so she pushed her handbag onto the floor and climbed across the passenger seat and tried the other side.

"Please. Please open." She clicked the handle and the door moved, opening wide enough for her to turn sideways in an awkward one-legged hop manoeuvre and pull herself out.

She closed her door and stashed the keys in her pocket. The wind was still moaning through the trees, but in the midst of the thick foliage she was partly protected. It was only when she reached the road that the gale hit her and tugged at her clothes.

Lucy stood for a moment, partially hidden behind a large gum. There was no sound on the road, save the shuddering trees and the whoosh of the squall as it blew across the bitumen. Her fingers were already red and numb from the cold. She rubbed her hands together then darted across the narrow road. Without hesitating she jogged the few metres to the stairs, boots crunching on the gravel as she skidded to a stop.

For a second the sight of the house took her breath away and she felt the same quiver of dread she'd experienced the day before. Only then she was leaving, scurrying for the safety of the car, eager to drive away. Now, as she was about to enter the ominous-looking fortress, Lucy had a moment of uncertainty. *What am I doing?*

Going in alone was a crazy idea. The lies Samson told about having a sister and what Roberta said about his birth defect were enough to convince her the man was unhinged. Then there was the drug operation. What did she think she was going to achieve by breaking into the man's house?

She glanced up at the second storey windows. Was it Tim she had seen yesterday? The wind tore at her hair, whipping it around her face like dark ribbons. Could she walk away without being sure?

"Damn." Lucy's voice was swallowed up by the gale. She had to be sure.

Once up the wide stone steps she headed to the right, following the curved wall around the side of the building. Instead of pressing the buzzer Lucy moved along the terrace, passing another set of glass doors. She paused and tried the handle, but the doors were sealed.

She kept moving, noting the curved driveway she'd spotted the day before. The wide gravel expanse snaked its way around the house and ended at a triple-bay garage.

The door was down, giving the place a blank, unoccupied feel. Lucy spotted a rutted track veering off to the side of the garage and wondered if it led to the field Damon had found. Maybe this was another way in and out of the plantation.

With her heart dashing against her ribs she turned back to the house and moved further around the building until the terrace opened up and the rear of the property was revealed. What was once a lawn was now a sea of deep grass and weeds shimmering in the wind. Amongst the wild greensward, a rusty slide sat at a lazy angle beside a rotted rope swing. As the gale buffeted the back of the house, the swing moved furiously back and forth, its one remaining cord clinging desperately to the limb of a bare jacaranda tree.

The garden reminded her of a grim poem: *And round about his home the glory that blushed and bloomed is but a dim-remembered story.* A shiver raced its way up Lucy's spine. She wondered what dim-remembered secrets this place kept. *Stop it. It's just an overgrown garden.* She ran her fingers through her wind-tangled hair and dragged her gaze away from the decaying lawn.

Double doors, wider than the ones on the side of the house, faced the garden as though waiting to be opened onto the fading grandeur that had once been a child's delight. *This place is making me crazy.* Lucy tried the doors expecting them to be locked. Instead, the lever turned with a grating whine and the door on the left jumped open a few centimetres.

She wasn't sure if she was relieved or disappointed. Part of her hoped the place would be sealed up like a whiskey vat, giving her no choice but turn tail and leave. Now that there was a way in, she couldn't give up until she knew her brother wasn't being kept somewhere inside the huge house.

Before entering she grabbed one last look at the sky. The clouds were piling up like dark smoke covering the sun. Night would fall early and within an hour the sky would be dark.

"I won't be here that long." She turned back to the door and slipped inside.

* * *

Ringing on the end of the line, echoey and cut by static, Damon gave up and ended the call. He'd tried Lucy's phone four times since leaving Busselton and every time it had gone to voicemail. With his phone close to dying he wrestled the wheel with one hand and pulled into the motel parking lot. The Saab was gone. Any last hope that she was back died when she refused to answer her phone.

He sat for a moment considering how to proceed. His first impulse was to drive straight to Nightmesser's house and find Lucy. He pulled the gun from under the seat and sat with it in his lap. But something she'd told him kept nagging at his thoughts and he wondered if they'd been missing something obvious all along. Whatever it was it would have to wait.

The phone's battery was almost spent. Still waiting for Larson's contact to call and with Lucy not answering, he couldn't afford to lose the phone. It would be dark in forty minutes. Somehow the world seemed more dangerous at night. He turned off the engine, pushed the gun back under the seat and jumped out of the Jeep.

He stepped into his room and something scrunched under his boot. In the fading light he stooped and picked up the sheet of paper. The words were shadowed and unreadable. Turning on the light, he scanned the sheet.

Lucy's writing was neat and sloping to the right. The message was short and to the point. She'd gone for coffee and would be back in half an hour. Yet between writing this note and the second message she'd left on his voicemail, Lucy decided to head to Nightmesser's house. What had led her to do something so impulsive?

Damon turned the paper over noticing she'd used the back of the letter from St Ruben's. His chest tightened. The thing that had been nagging at him since leaving Larson's office clicked into place like a latch falling into its housing. He didn't believe in coincidences even after his weirdly fortuitous meeting with Lucy on the road, but here he was staring at the very thing he'd been trying to put his finger on. Roberta Stemms' son. Lucy told him the old lady mentioned not liking her son spending time with Samson. If Roberta had a son, why wasn't he the one the hospital was writing to? And if the old lady's boy was still in contact with Samson, maybe he knew something.

"Shit." If Lucy hadn't gone off on her own he'd have had time to follow the lead.

Ready to turn and rush back to the Jeep, Damon almost forgot why he'd come into the room. He crossed the floor in two strides and pulled the charger out of his pack. Still holding the letter, he headed back to the car.

With the engine running and the phone charging he should have been on the road. Every nerve in his body was ringing with the need to move, but still he hesitated. The thing with the old lady's son could be nothing. He ran his hand over the base of his neck. It was probably a minor detail, something to be followed up in a quiet moment, but even as he rationalised it he wasn't convinced. His instincts told him there was something there. Something vital.

Torn between the need for action and the certainty Nightmesser wasn't acting alone, Damon unfolded the sheet of paper and dialled St Ruben's.

* * *

There had been no sign of an alarm when Samson Nightmesser let Lucy into the house the day before, but that didn't mean there wasn't one tucked discreetly into an unseen alcove. Turning and pulling the terrace door closed, she took a leap of faith and stepped into the room.

Waiting, almost holding her breath expecting the shrill of a siren, she took a few more tentative steps. Somewhere in the depths of the house a clock ticked. Lucy blew out a heavy breath and let some of the tension drop from her shoulders. The late afternoon light trickled through the lace curtains that cloaked the double doors, playing a shadowy pattern on a long table and hulking furniture all draped in white sheets. The room appeared to be some sort of dining area.

Like the garden, this space seemed abandoned; even the air tasted stale and dusty on her lips. She hurried past the covered furniture and through an archway that led to the kitchen. The room was mostly bare, save a raw-wood table that looked like something used in an old-fashioned butcher's shop. Deep double basins were set into the bench top. Opaque glass and panelling on the cupboards gave the room an art deco feel. Yet like everything else at the rear of the property, the kitchen was faded and unused. *If Samson's raking in the drug money, he's not spending it on the house.*

Lucy's boots padded on the tiled floor, the soft sound conspicuous in the silence as she crossed to a doorway. Her skin was hot like she'd already been caught in the act of breaking the law. She pushed through the door and was relieved to find herself in the foyer. The sharp chemical odour she remembered from the day before hung in the air. The smell was so pungent she wrinkled her nose and stifled a cough. Around her the startling artwork covered the walls in a helter skelter collection of distorted bodies.

The idea of Samson painting the disturbing snatches of body parts while believing himself to be his sister sent a rash of goosebumps across Lucy's already burning skin. She didn't want to be in the house any longer than absolutely necessary. The idea made her jittery. She thought of checking the time and realised she didn't have her handbag. Her stomach contracted as if from a physical blow. In her almost acrobatic struggle to get out of the car she'd left her bag on the floor of the vehicle.

"Fuck." The curse echoed up the wide staircase, making her feel small and vulnerable in the vast house.

She could back out, rush back to the car and wait for Damon. But his unfailing logic would throw up roadblocks, forcing her to rethink the notion of rushing in to search the house. And there might not be another chance like this. Seeing Samson on the street, knowing the house was empty was an opportunity she couldn't let go. No, Tim might be here and she wasn't leaving until she had looked for him. He was depending on her. He'd always depended on her and she'd never let him down.

Unshed tears were twisting in the back of her throat. She was afraid. Afraid of being caught, but more terrified of never knowing what happened to Tim. She needed to find her brother alive or dead. *Let him be alive*. Not allowing herself a faltering step, she moved to the stairs and started to climb.

Upstairs the landing split left and right. The chemical smell was stronger, almost overpowering. The doors on the far left and far right looked to be the most likely to house windows facing the front of the building. She closed her eyes for a heartbeat and pictured the curtains as they twitched. It was the left side of the house, she was sure of it.

Passing a few doors and a small hallway, Lucy moved to the far room. The landing was carpeted with runners, patterned and thick. Like the stairs, they absorbed any sound. She paused at the door, fingers curled around the knob.

"Tim?" Her heart jumped as she turned the knob.

Clearly a bedroom. The space was cluttered and in disarray. The details were difficult to make out with only splashes of dim light creeping through the edges of the heavy curtains. The stench of sweat and burnt food permeated the air. Lucy noticed a small electric hotplate set

154

up on an aging coffee table. The makeshift cooking station was stacked with dirty plates and bowls, and a blackened saucepan caked with something crusty and sour smelling.

"Jesus." Lucy grimaced, taking in the unmade bed and piles of books cast randomly on every available surface.

Someone was using the room, and by the look and smell, living in this one space. Atop a stack of books, she spotted a shoe box stuffed with photographs.

Touching the old images made her skin crawl as the edges of each picture felt grimy. Tim wasn't in the room, nor did she think he had been. There was no time to waste. She had to move on, keep searching while Samson was occupied. Yet despite the feeling of revulsion she couldn't resist flicking through the photos.

Old coloured pictures of Samson and his father taken in various settings. Many of the images were of the garden, showing its former glory and always with Samson sitting on the swing or perched on the slide or kicking a football. The pictures looked staged. On close inspection the little boy's face looked sullen and disinterested.

Lucy picked through another stack and found a picture of a young woman, a pretty face smiling into the camera. Even years later and crumpled by age, Lucy recognised the woman as Roberta Stemms. She wore a light blue uniform and apron, the fabric strained across her belly.

For a moment Lucy was confused, but then she remembered the way the old lady had called Samson's father Nathan. There was a familiarity and affection in the way Roberta used the man's name. Could it be that there was more between Roberta and Nathan than a working relationship?

Lucy dropped the photographs then quickly arranged them back in what she hoped was the correct order.

There was a clock on the bedside table. It was almost four o'clock. Time was running away and she'd found no trace of her brother. She left the room and closed the door behind her.

On the other side of the landing she cracked open an identical door. The first thing that hit her was the smell, a cloying mix of chemicals, paint, and something heavy and sweet. Stepping through the doorway, she felt her pulse jump and the air leave her lungs.

The large space was made smaller by the chaos of the makeshift studio complete with rows of half-completed paintings and a huge covered easel that sat amidst pink furnishings, stuffed toys and feminine debris. Like the other room, the area was cluttered, only here there was something frantic in the disorder.

Lucy took a few steps into the room, her gaze drawn by the dressing table. A mannequin head wearing a long blonde wig sat amongst a mess of make-up and lotions. Someone had drawn a face on the blank foam dummy head. A smear of red lipstick created a crooked mouth below wide black eyes ringed with blue eye shadow. The effect was somehow aggressive and crude at the same time.

As Lucy stepped closer she caught something reflected in the mirror from the far wall, and a tremor ran through her limbs. She'd been so focused on the dressing table and strange, adolescent furnishings that she hadn't noticed the wall alongside the door.

The wide expanse of white plaster was littered with images, small white-bordered prints immediately recognisable as instamatic photographs. Red marker lines and scrawls snaked their way through the pictures. Lucy walked towards the wall on legs that were numb, her boots scuffing the bare floor.

Eyes shifting back and forth between stark, brutal images, she covered her mouth trying to stifle a sob. A macabre collage of young men, shirtless and in various stages of abuse and malnutrition decorated the wall. Names and descriptions were scrawled around the photos: Tyson – soulful and bitter, Andrew – bold and dangerous.

So many young men. Lucy couldn't stop the tears. The ghoulish cruelty overwhelmed her and she turned away. Dozens of paintings leaned against the wall under the window. More canvases were balanced against a bookcase. She couldn't escape the bombardment of images. And then the words on the wall and the painting came together like a collision in Lucy's brain. They weren't descriptions scrawled alongside the photos, but names. Names she or he'd given the paintings.

All those angles, the stark limbs and bodies were tortured young men. Every ounce of warmth seemed to melt from Lucy's body, leaving her shivering. Was this Tim's fate? She had to know.

Forcing herself back to the wall, she scanned the sickening images, checking off names. Some familiar, the ones in Damon's file and other new names, more than they had imagined. At least six, but no sign of Tim. Relief like a wash of hope came and just as quickly vanished under the realisation that she was glad the men in the photos weren't her brother. She'd actually felt a moment of elation before her stomach soured, knowing these men were someone else's family. Someone else's loved ones.

Lucy turned in a circle, scanning the horrific studio. If her brother wasn't amongst the men on the wall then where was he? The disgust and shock that gripped her turned to something duskier. Panic tinted with darkness, like the strange pigments in the paintings, flooded her mind.

She wanted to find her brother and hurt Samson Nightmesser, make him feel pain and loss. Lucy ran to the cupboard near the bed and pulled open the door. A row of women's clothing, large and old-fashioned, bunched tightly on the rack. She wasn't sure what she was looking for, but there had to be something that told her where the men were kept. The kind of torture she'd seen in the photos needed privacy and time. The house was big—too big to search in the dwindling minutes. Then there was the surrounding property and the wilderness that stretched for countless kilometres.

She touched one of the dresses. The thick cotton felt coarse on her fingers. She could leave now and go to the police, ring Matt and have him send a crew to Night Town. There was enough evidence in the room to warrant a major investigation, taking local involvement out of the picture. But something stopped her. She could almost hear Damon's voice deep and calm whispering in her ear. *Nightmesser will go to prison, but once he's in custody he might clam up.* Like so many before him: killers who'd taken their victims' whereabouts to the grave, Samson could refuse to reveal Tim's location.

"I should have waited for you." She spoke aloud, like Damon was standing beside her. Coming alone was a crazy risk. If she'd waited just another hour or so… "You would have talked me out of it."

She looked down and noticed a box nestled between six large pairs of women's shoes. She crouched and pulled it forward, noting its weight and the clinking of glass. The only other sound was the gale whistling around the house, shaking the windows as it gathered strength. The chemical smell was stronger in the small closet space; like vinegar, only laced with something sweet.

The lid was decorated with pictures cut from magazines: gorgeous young male models shirtless and posing seductively. The glossy photos cropped and pasted around a piece of card. *For Memories' Sake.* The words were written in large letters using some sort of glitter pen. The box looked like the work of a teenage girl, but Lucy knew better. This was Samantha's work.

Lucy swallowed, pushing the dread down until it churned in her stomach. Unaware of the wind as it swamped the noise of an approaching engine, she opened the lid. She wasn't sure what she'd been expecting, but definitely not a collection of jars. Six containers, glass with silver screw-top lids like pickled onion jars. Lucy held her breath to avoid inhaling the chemical smell and pulled a jar from the box.

Murky liquid sloshed as she held the container up and turned it so the fading afternoon light played on the glass. It was difficult to see what the canister contained. Something drifted in the solution. Something flat and irregularly shaped. Lucy jerked her wrist, making the object turn lazily until it became visible.

For an instant she was confused and then the pattern became clear, revealing a snake's head. Lucy's wrist trembled and the glass almost slipped from her fingers. Realisation spread over her like a hot flush. The young guy in Damon's file, Andrew. She was staring at his tattoo – his skin.

Lucy dropped the jar back into the box and slammed the lid in place. Her mind was jumping from the horrid discovery to the pictures on the wall. This room, Samantha, the jars: it was too much, an overload of madness and evil. She had to get out before Samson returned. The chamber of nightmares that was his life seemed to be like a living thing, surrounding Lucy with malevolence and danger. The air was thick and hot and suffocating.

She stood ready to bolt for the stairs when the sound of a car door slamming froze her to her spot. A few seconds later a metallic creak. With her hand on the closet door she listened. It was almost impossible to be sure, but she thought she heard shoes crunching on the gravel. Not knowing if Samson would enter from the front or back of the house, she was paralysed with fear. The man she'd interviewed only yesterday was capable of unspeakable things. She had seen the evidence on the walls and in the jars. It didn't matter if he committed those acts as himself or Samantha. Once he got inside the house, she would be trapped with him.

A door slammed somewhere in the building. Lucy's chest tightened and her pulse filled her ears. *What now?*

159

Could she risk making a run for the terrace doors? Maybe the element of surprise could work in her favour. Samson wouldn't be expecting her to come thundering down the stairs. But he was deranged, dangerous beyond anything she could have imagined. The thought of crossing his path made her weak with fear.

In the seconds she stood agonising over what to do he had reached the stairs. Even with the thick runner she heard the creak of the old boards as he climbed to the second floor. On impulse she darted into the closet and pulled the door closed behind her.

Pushing to the left and stepping around the macabre box and Nightmesser's oversized shoes, she wedged herself into the corner behind the tightly packed rack of clothes. She crouched slightly, trying to make herself as small as possible.

Time ticked by, maybe five minutes, and nothing. The light under the door dimmed as the sun set. Apart from the wind there was no sound in the room. Lucy's breathing slowed slightly as some of the terror receded. Samson wasn't in the room. She'd heard no sound since the creak of the stairs. *Maybe he's in the other bedroom.* She wasn't sure how DID worked. But after seeing the two bedrooms she believed Nightmesser had two distinct personalities. Samson's room was dirty and depressing, somewhere an introverted hoarder would dwell while Samantha's room was colourful, frantic and terrifying. If she had to guess, Lucy would say Samantha was the more dangerous of the two. What she couldn't work out was how often Samantha's personality emerged.

Not sure of how much time she had before Nightmesser would become Samantha, she decided it was time to go. She moved slowly, trying not to disturb anything in the closet as she stepped around the crowded floor.

Pushing the door open, Lucy stepped out of the closet and back into the room. Outside, the sun was almost gone, the dying rays cast elongated shadows of bruised light into the room. She moved carefully, eager to get to the door, but unable to resist one last glance at the wall of photos.

In the gloom, the young men were little more than dark blurs. She prayed that for Tim's and all the men's families' sake she could get out of the house and bring help. But as she turned to leave, her boot caught the edge of the canvas that covered the easel. With a whoosh the cover dropped, revealing a half-completed work.

A shriek escaped before Lucy could cover her mouth. Tim's features were unmistakable even in the dusky light, his green eyes stared out of a bruised face and with one arm cast over his head as if to protect himself.

"Oh God. Oh no. Tim." Lucy couldn't control the words as they ran out of her mouth. An instamatic photo was clipped to the top left corner of the painting.

She should have been running, but her legs were bending like the floor was pulling her down. She grabbed at the easel to steady herself and the whole frame rocked. As she scrambled to steady the painting, one of the easel's legs landed with a *thump*. The clatter was unbearably loud and sudden.

Lucy snatched the small photo off the painting and turned to the door. She didn't bother to try and disguise her footfalls; the damage was already done. As she reached the door she heard another door open.

"Who's there?" Samson voice sounded gruff and loud.

Lucy pulled the door open and sprinted onto the landing. On the far side of the second storey she saw Nightmesser, his head poking out of the other bedroom door, his mouth agape in surprise. Before he could react, she bolted for the stairs and was descending in a series of jumps and stumbles.

"Stop. Don't move." Samson was after her now. She could hear his shouts and the clamour of his footsteps.

She sped up, not daring to look behind her. Like a charging rhinoceros, she rushed down the hall, collided with the swinging door and burst into the kitchen. Unable to stop her speeding momentum, she hit the raw-wood table. The impact knocked the air out of her lungs with an *oomph*. Dazed but fuelled by sheer panic, she turned right and skidded across the tile floor.

Behind her, the swinging door flapped open, but Lucy didn't hesitate. She rounded the covered furniture and tore open the terrace door, stumbling out of the house into near darkness. The air when it hit her lungs was fresh and clean, washing away the chemical smell that burned in her mouth. As she ran for the front of the building she realised she still had the small photograph clutched in her hand, so she stuffed it in her coat pocket and kept moving.

I did it. I'm out. She felt a burst of elation as she crossed the gravelled path and sprinted into the cul-de-sac only to find herself pinned under harsh light as a police car blocked the road. With nowhere to run, Lucy stopped and held her hand up to shield her eyes from the glare as the windstorm whaled around her.

In the cover of red and blue light, a car door opened. "What's the rush?" Senior Constable Holsey's disembodied voice echoed out of the wash of lights.

* * *

"Is Mrs Stemms expecting your call?" The receptionist's voice carried just the right amount of cheerful curiosity.

Damon didn't hesitate. "Yes. My associate, Lucy, visited Mrs Stemms this afternoon and told her to expect my call." He paused. "It's a family matter... It's about Mrs Stemms' son."

"Oh, I see. Yes, I'll put you through to her room, but let it ring." She gave a short laugh. "It might take her caregiver a minute or so to pick up."

"Thanks," Damon said, and waited while the call was transferred.

He watched the rear-view mirror as he listened to the phone ringing. The sun was setting, the sky swarming with grey clouds as the wind rocked his stationary car.

"Hello. Mrs Stemms' room." The female voice sounded tired and overworked.

Damon ran through the same explanation he'd given the receptionist, including the mention of the old lady's son. There was a slight hesitation before the woman's curt response. "Just a minute." Damon heard a voice, muffled like the caregiver had clamped the phone to her chest.

The murmuring continued and was followed by rustling. "Hello?" The tremulous word was enough to tell him the caregiver had given the old lady the phone.

Damon hadn't had much time to prepare what he was going to say, and from what Lucy told him, Roberta was still quite switched on. He could feel the tension in his body winding its way up his arm until he was gripping the phone like a gun. He didn't want to frighten the elderly woman, so he tried to keep his voice casual and friendly. "Hi, my friend Lucy came to see you today. She told me she really enjoyed chatting with you."

More rustling. For a second he thought she'd dropped the phone, but then, "Oh yes. You mean Sammy's secretary?"

"Yes." Damon forced his grip to relax. "That's right. She works for Mr Nightmesser."

"I'm glad Sammy has someone helping him." Roberta sounded at ease, eager to chat, so Damon didn't interrupt. "He always used to get himself in a state over the smallest things. But I suppose that was partly Nathan's fault. He was so hard on Sammy." She made a clicking sound with her tongue. "One time my Gordon hid one of his favourite magazines. Oh... what was it called... one of those sport things." He could hear her breathing and wondered if she'd nodded off.

"Mrs Stemms?"

"Yes? What was I saying?" She sounded sleepy, like her tongue was tired.

He was losing her, so he tried to jump the conversation forward. "You were telling me about your son, Gordon. Is he still living in Night Town?"

"Sure, he never goes far, but I'm not sure if he's there now or... Sammy might know. Have you asked Sammy?"

"Yes, that's right. Lucy did mention something about Gordon." Damon's chest tightened. Gordon was a common enough name. There had to be at least a few guys with the same name in Night Town.

"Ah... there you are. I knew he'd be around. They were never good for each other, but..." She stretched out the word. "There was a connection." Mrs Stemms' voice, already wavering, sounded tearful. "It wasn't Gordon's fault. He was so much younger." She sniffed before continuing. "He doesn't visit me, you know. He was so angry about me and Nathan." She let out a sigh. "It was a long time ago. I don't know why I'm going on about it."

Her mind was jumping from one thing to another so Damon tried to keep her on track. "I understand. It must be upsetting for you – Gordon not visiting."

"It's probably better this way." Roberta suddenly sounded more alert. "Gordon was always a handful. I don't think I could cope with all that now. And... well, we did nothing wrong. Nathan was a widower and I was still Holsey then. I wasn't married so it wasn't wrong. Not when you think what the young ones these days get up to. But Gordon was jealous. Black-hearted with anger."

Holsey. Damon's hand was gripping the phone again so tightly he was surprised it didn't break in his fist. He knew Nightmesser wasn't acting alone. All this time they'd been looking for a lead on Samson's accomplice and he'd been right there staring them in the face all along. *No*, his heart hammered against his ribs. Not them. Lucy. Gordon Holsey had been in *Lucy's* face all along.

He shook his head like he was trying to wake up from a nightmare. Roberta was still talking, but Damon was no longer listening. "Mrs Stemms," he broke in on what she was saying. "I have to go." He hung up without waiting for a reply.

The engine was still running so he dropped it into gear and pulled out of the parking lot. It was almost 4:30 p.m. He had no idea how long Lucy had been at Nightmesser's house. The voicemail came in at around four o'clock, so she could have been at the house for over half an hour. A string of curses ran through his mind. Lucy was smart and she could look after herself, but between Nightmesser and the cop, Holsey, she might be way out of her depth.

Chapter Fifteen

Pinned in the light, Lucy glanced back towards the house and noticed Samson was nowhere in sight. He might have called the police, but that wouldn't explain how Holsey got to the house so quickly. *He could have been nearby. It's a small town.* It was feasible, but she didn't think so.

"I…" She thought of telling the cop what she'd seen, but Damon's warning about the local police being involved stopped her. "I was trying to speak to Mr Nightmesser." She let her arms hang at her sides. "Just, you know, get an interview."

Holsey stepped out of the light and walked towards her. She had the urge to run just as she'd done in the house. She even snatched a look towards the bush, wondering if she could disappear into the dense foliage before the senior constable reached her.

"Where's your car?"

The question took her by surprise, pulling her attention back from the possible escape route. Of all the things Holsey could have asked, this seemed an unlikely question. Not wanting to reveal the fact that she'd hidden her car, she saw an opportunity.

"My friend dropped me here. He'll be back soon to pick me up." She could hear the quake in her voice and hoped he hadn't noticed.

He was closer now, crossing the distance between them with unwavering confidence, his heavy shoes almost silent on the bitumen. "Looks like tracks heading into the bush." He jerked his head to the other side of the cul-de-sac as a gale lifted his sparse hair. "Like someone drove in there recently. If I go in there and have a look, will I see that fancy car of yours?" His voice was relaxed, almost conversational, but as he drew near, Lucy could see the predatory look in his pale eyes.

He stopped a metre or so away from her and she realised any chance of running was gone. With the light behind him he appeared larger, more imposing.

"I… No. As I said, my fr—"

"I can't have you running around out here bothering Mr Nightmesser."

"No, I was only—"

He held up a hand, the movement sudden like he meant to strike her. Lucy flinched and took a backward step. "Don't interrupt." There was a smile on his face now, he appeared to be pleased by her reaction, in knowing he was intimidating her. "As I was trying to say." He leaned his head forward, punctuating the words with each movement of his neck. "I can't have you running around out here. I'll take you back to town." He turned and spread one arm wide, indicating the police car. "Hop in."

Her mind was racing, keeping time with her thundering heartbeat. She tried to think of something to say, a reason not to accept the lift. But Holsey's face was set in porcine determination, and one hand was hooked casually on his hip, his fingers brushing the handle of his gun.

She swallowed, the movement made almost impossible by the lack of saliva in her mouth. The early evening air seemed to carry a charge and she wondered if it was coming from the windstorm or rolling off Holsey in waves of barely contained violence.

"Okay." She walked past him, steeling herself in preparation for an attack.

How many times had she interviewed women – damaged, victimised women? She'd sympathised with them, but could never understand how they had allowed themselves to be forced into situations they knew would end in violence. She had always been so sure there had been a way these women could have resisted, and now here she was obediently walking towards Holsey's car while every nerve in her body screamed at her to run or fight or do anything but get inside.

She reached for the back door, but Holsey was at her side. "No." He opened the front passenger door. "Up front with me."

His breath smelled of cheese as he crowded her into the car. She could see herself pushing past him and running, picking up speed until he was left behind panting on the road. Inside her head she was screaming, but still she complied. Sliding into the car, she saw her last chance of escape disappearing as her limbs refused to snap into action.

"Good girl." As Holsey slammed the door, trapping her inside the car, she caught a glimpse of his shoes: camel-coloured boots with black trim at the ankles. His words were reverberating in Lucy's skull like a contrecoup brain injury, hitting one side first and then striking the opposite side of her brain.

Those two words, *good girl*, used so soothingly like she was an obedient child. *Good girl. Good girl.* The words or maybe recognising the boots from the CCTV footage, shattered the spell and she was moving. She was flinging the door open and springing from the car. The night air was like welcoming arms as she pushed off the car half expecting to feel a bullet cut through her flesh.

"Whoa. No, you don't." Holsey, half way around the vehicle, darted back and made a grab for her.

Lucy ducked her head to avoid his arm and plunged into the road. The gale pulling at her open coat slowed her progress as she zigged left and made for the trees. One, two steps, and she was pulled back like a dog caught on a leash. Holsey had her coat and was dragging her to a halt. Lucy let out a cry of frustration and twisted to the right, dropping her shoulders and letting her arms slide free from the puffer.

As she freed herself of the coat, Holsey's arm came around her body and lifted her off the road. The coat fluttered in the wind and sank to the bitumen as he half-carried her back to the open car door.

"Get the fuck inside." He took hold of her hair and jerked her into the car.

Lucy felt her scalp lift, and a clump of hair tear free. She let out another scream, this one a mixture of pain and anger. He was panting, his face shiny with sweat.

"If you try that again." He wiped his nose on the back of his hand as he leaned into the passenger side. "I'll break your jaw."

"Where's my brother?" Her scalp was on fire and there were tears in her eyes, making it difficult to see his face.

He slammed the door and she heard the lock *ping*. In the seconds it took him to round the car and jump in the driver's side, Lucy wiped her eyes and scanned the cab for anything that might work as a weapon. There was a pen on the console, so she grabbed it and shoved it in the pocket of her jeans.

The locks opened with a dull click and Holsey climbed in, the car dipping under his weight. With the interior light on Lucy could see the radio was turned off. For a second he just stared straight ahead seeming to be watching something in the dark.

He lurched in the seat and Lucy jumped, pressing her body against the passenger door. Holsey barked out a short laugh and pulled his phone out of his pants pocket. "Jumpy." His tone was teasing, he was enjoying her fear.

Hating the way he made her cower, she straightened up in the seat. "There's a news crew coming to town tomorrow. I've told my producer everything." She watched his face for a reaction, but he seemed intent on his phone. "He knows about the missing men and the drugs." She was breathless, fear and panic flooding her body with adrenalin.

Holsey looked up from the screen and placed a thick finger to his lips, made a *shhh* sound, then put the phone to his ear. As he lifted his arm she could see a dark circle of sweat on his shirt.

"It's me. There's a problem." Holsey's gruff voice filled the car. He glanced over at her. "Yeah, the reporter." He nodded like the person on the other end of the phone could see him. "Yep. I'll see you there." He cut the call and shoved the phone back in his pocket.

"My friend will be looking for me. He knows I came here." She could hear her voice rising. "This is crazy. You can't think you're going to get away with it? There's—"

His hand shot out with suddenness she hadn't seen coming. He grasped the side of her head and slammed it against the passenger window with a short *thump* that rocked the car and sent a burst of pain into the left side of her skull. Lucy's teeth chomped together at the impact and she heard a crack. Stunned, eyes blurred with dark spots, she grasped her head in her hands.

She heard a humming and wasn't sure if it was coming from inside her head or if he'd started the car. When she looked up they were moving. She ran her hand over her head, fingers probing a rapidly rising lump where she'd hit the window.

"You wanted to know where your brother is?" His voice was loud. Loud and hollow, like he was speaking into a tunnel. "If you're a very good girl, I'll take you to him." His words were getting clearer, but the stabbing in Lucy's skull continued. "But," he said and turned his washed-out eyes on her. "You have to stop yammering on at me. I don't like it when you make threats, okay?" He sounded surprisingly normal, almost reasonable, and Lucy found herself nodding in spite of the pain when her head moved.

He drove slowly along Nightmesser's driveway and then veered right onto the dirt track Lucy had noticed earlier. Her stomach clenched and something sour threatened to climb its way up her throat. Any hope she had of signalling another car or jumping out at a stop sign vanished. They were heading into the darkness. The only illumination came from the headlights and the moon half-cloaked in dark clouds.

$$* * *$$

The shrill of the phone startled his attention off the road and for an instant the Jeep weaved to the left. Damon grabbed the phone from the console. Snatching glances between the road and the mobile, he saw the caller's number was blocked.

"Hello?" Damon put the call on speaker and set it down in the console.

"Larson Granger passed on your details." The sentence gave little away but Damon understood the caller was an undercover officer and had to be cautious.

"Yes. But I can't wait on your cloak and dagger shit. I need help now. I'm on my way to Samson Nightmesser's house, my…" He hesitated, not sure what to call Lucy. "My associate has gone missing."

There was a pause on the end of the line. "Jesus. Are you talking about Lucy?"

Damon drew up to the town's only traffic light and picked up the phone. "How do you know about Lucy?" He'd heard about UCOs but had never actually met one. If this guy was on the inside, he might be able to get to Lucy before anything happened. *If it hasn't already*.

"Don't go anywhere near Nightmesser's house," the UCO said, avoiding the question. "If you do, you'll be compromising a long-running investigation. You don't want to get mixed up with these people. This is a big operation, bigger than you can imagine." There was tension in the man's voice. "This isn't something you just walk into, trust me."

"Sorry," Damon snapped back. "I don't know you and I'm already on my way." He was tempted to end the call. The UCO obviously knew about the plantation. He wondered if the missing men were just collateral damage in what the UCO had discovered so far.

"Look, if you interfere with this, you could be charged with obstructing an investigation. Leave this with me and I'll…" The UCO paused and Damon wondered if the man had any idea about the missing men.

"You'll what? Wait until her body turns up?" He was angry now, the emotion fuelled by worry and fear for Lucy's safety. The light had changed and Damon realised he was still sitting there. Behind him, a horn blared.

He was driving again. Not waiting for an answer from the faceless cop, he plunged on. "Do you realise how many men have gone missing around Night Town in the last six years? Five including Tim. And those are just the ones I've come across." He should have hung up, but the heat of his anger needed to be vented and right now the cop was his target. "Have you guys even bothered to look into any of that or would that have compromised your investigation?"

"I'm only aware of Tim Hush's disappearance. I didn't know there were others… And you can't be sure that any of that is linked to this case. This has never been about missing persons, not until Lucy started asking questions." There was a pause, the cop's breathing coming through the speaker and filling the Jeep.

"And now you know." Damon was approaching the bridge. He'd be at Nightmesser's in fifteen minutes, less if he floored the accelerator.

"All right. I'll meet you at Nightmesser's. My name's Brock Day. Don't do anything until I get there."

Damon picked up the phone. "You'd better hurry, Brock. I'm not waiting." He cut the call and dropped the phone back into the console.

* * *

With every rock and jump on the track, Lucy's gut churned as waves of nausea rose and fell. The air in the car was heavy with the stench of sweat and cheese, a combination of which seemed to ooze from Holsey's pores. As much as she dreaded their destination, part of her was desperate for the stomach-roiling ride to be over.

They drove in silence, save the wind whipping around the vehicle with a ghostly whistle, and Holsey's nasal breathing. At one point he glanced up at the rear-view mirror and Lucy thought she saw the reflection of lights play over his face. If someone was following them in the dark, Holsey seemed calm about it.

She wanted to turn and see if she could make out a vehicle, but Holsey's eyes bounced back and forth from the track to her face. There was an unspoken threat in his pale gaze that kept her pinned to the spot like a child under the steely eyes of an angry teacher. The needle-like pain in her head and burning scalp were a reminder of how sudden and vicious his attacks could be. They'd been driving for almost ten minutes when the car slowed and the headlights played over a building.

In the shower of light Lucy made out a stone structure with a tall, sharply-angled roof. The headlights bleached the building a dirty grey, making the walls look grim and austere. It was an inhospitable place, isolated and eerie in the darkness. A line of sweat broke out on the base of her neck and she could feel her fingernails biting into the flesh of her palms.

"That's the original house." Holsey's voice was a sudden shock in the silence. He veered right and came to a stop. "End of the road." He used the same conversational tone he'd employed while threatening to break her jaw.

He turned in his seat so he was facing her. "My great grandfather built this place. Not that any of it belongs to me." There was an edge of bitterness in his tone now. "The old man didn't mind knocking up my mother. He just didn't want to marry her." He shrugged, his beefy shoulders edging up to his ears.

Lucy was trying to follow what he was saying, but was having difficulty dragging her eyes away from the old house and the way the long grass shuddered in the wind. She couldn't stop her mind from throwing up images of the young men in Damon's file. Had this been the last place they'd seen? *Is this where he brought Tim?*

"So… so your mother is…" Her head was spinning, dark blotches dancing in and out of sight.

He was nodding. "Yeah, I know you went to see her. The old people's home called Sammy and told him all about your visit. Don't worry, he went along with your secretary story. No point in causing a shitstorm at the oldie's home." He waggled a finger near her face and she shrank back against the door. "You're a smart one, I'll give you that. But not smart enough to leave town when I told you to. I thought my late-night visit to your room at the pub might have done the trick, but no. That's too bad." He laughed; a sharp cruel sound. "Too bad for you."

Behind them came the sound of an engine and the hiss and crackle of tyres over leaves and twigs. A car door opened and closed. Lucy thought she heard a second door slam, but couldn't be sure of her own ears, at least not with her pulse roaring and a line of fire drilling her brain.

Holsey opened his door and climbed out of the vehicle. Lucy turned and watched him disappear around the back of the car. This was it. If she let them take her into the eerie-looking building, she would never come out again. He hadn't locked the door so she could jump out and run. Outside of the headlights, the moon was clouded so she could disappear into the darkness. If she made it that far without being shot or caught, she might stand a chance.

There were voices, Holsey's and another. Her first thought was Samson but the other voice was too high and feminine to belong to Nightmesser. Unless... Lucy's heart spasmed. Unless it's Samantha. Somehow the idea of Nightmesser's 'sister' was more terrifying than Holsey with all his brutish violence.

Lucy put her hand on the latch and tried to open the door with as little noise as possible. The sweat gathering on her neck trickled down her spine in a cold line. As she pulled up on the latch, a face filled the window. Lucy jerked back, her fingers losing their grip on the door. For a heartbeat she felt relief at the familiar face and then confusion.

"Get out." The librarian. Lucy searched her memory for a name as the woman pulled the door open.

The wind blew the woman's short red hair up into wild spikes. Behind her the building with its pointed roof, blank windows and wide, dark door sat in almost complete darkness. Lucy sat unmoving as the icy air flew into the car. *Ruth*, Lucy's confused mind threw up the name.

"Are you deaf?" Ruth's tone was impatient, irritated. When Lucy didn't move, the woman grabbed her arm, her bony fingers digging through Lucy's woollen jumper. "Get out." Ruth pulled and Lucy stumbled out of the car.

"You're the librarian." It was a stupid thing to say, but Lucy's mind was having trouble working through the scene.

Ruth held something in her hand, a long brown pole of some kind. Lucy looked around and saw Holsey standing next to a woman with blonde hair, her long skirt wrapped against her legs by the wind. Only when the woman glanced her way and Lucy looked into her pale eyes did she realise it was Samantha.

Garish make-up and stark gold hair against Samson Nightmesser's aging face gave him a ghoulish appearance. Lucy felt a quiver in her knees, deep in the joints, making it seem like her legs were melting out from under her. The three of them surrounded her, Ruth with her drawn, angry lips, Holsey hulking and sullen, and Samantha. There was something bitter and hungry in Samantha's eyes.

Ruth was the first to speak. "You two have had your fun. Now we need to get this mess cleaned up." She jerked her chin at the building, speaking with authority as though used to giving orders.

Samantha tossed her head, sweeping the tousled blonde locks over her shoulder against the wind. "Gordon." The voice was high and exaggerated in its femininity. "It's impossible. Not until I finish the piece I'm working on." She was looking at Holsey, her long fingers wringing.

Holsey shrugged. "Ruth's right, Sammy. It's too risky now." Lucy was surprised by the gentleness in Holsey's voice. "Just let things calm down and we'll try again."

Try again? He was talking about her brother. Nightmesser was talking about her brother. They spoke with indifference, like Tim were a piece of clay, something to be used and then dumped or as Ruth said, *a mess*. It was too much to bear. Lucy could feel her emotions breaking loose. Fear wrapped in anger burnt its way through her jagged nerves.

"You're talking about my brother, you evil bastards." Her voice was shrill and twanging with contempt. "You make me sick." Staring at their startled faces, she searched for something hateful to say, something that would wound them in any small way. When nothing came to mind she drew back and spat. It was the first time in Lucy's life she'd ever actually spat on someone. In the following seconds she was as surprised as the people watching her. A wad of saliva landed on Ruth, hanging in her carrot-coloured hair like wet snow.

"You little bitch." Ruth's mouth dropped open with surprise, the ends turned down in disgust. She stepped forward and struck Lucy with the back of her hand, her knuckles crunching against Lucy's cheekbone.

The blow rocked Lucy's head and sent her stumbling against the car. Spitting on the woman was a futile act, but Lucy felt a spark of satisfaction as she steadied herself on the police car.

"Turn the lights on." Ruth was giving orders again. "We need to get a move on." She turned to Lucy and held the brown pole so it was close to Lucy's face. "See this." She clicked something and the pole gave a static buzz. The two prongs on the end closest to Lucy sizzled and a spark danced between copper teeth. "Cattle prod. Hurts like Christ." Ruth bared her teeth and a spray of breath, heavy with the stench of cigarettes and coffee, blasted Lucy's face. "Try anything clever and you'll find out what it feels like to be a cow."

"Come on." Holsey motioned with his head for his sister to follow. Holsey in his police uniform approached the building with Samantha tripping along in ridiculously clunky heels at his shoulder. There was a jingle of keys followed by a metal-on-metal creak. Seconds later lights glowed around the door and boarded up windows.

Lucy fixed her gaze on Ruth. "Is my brother in there?" The cold was working its way into her bones, making her teeth chatter as she spoke.

Ruth's blue eyes were red-rimmed, appearing to be raw with irritation. She lowered the prod and seemed to be thinking while weighing up her answer. Finally a smile, very different from the one she used at the library, crept across her gaunt face. "Not for much longer."

The words were like a punch, socking the wind out of Lucy's lungs and leaving her struggling for breath. Tim was inside the desolate building. How long had he been alone in this hellish place? Her little brother who loved the beach and could spend hours taking an old watch apart was being kept like an animal in the dark. The instamatic image she'd snatched from the painting jumped into her mind, Tim's eyes puffy and bruised, his sweet face barely recognisable.

Lucy gulped in a breath, letting the cold air fill her lungs. Ruth was watching her, the cattle prod dangling at her side. *I might never see him again.* The knowledge was crushing, almost paralysing. *I might never hear his voice. But he can hear mine. He can hear me and know he's not alone.*

She threw back her head and screamed. "Tim! Tim!" She was still screaming when Ruth jammed the prod into her shoulder and Lucy's muscles twisted into a knot of white fire.

Chapter Sixteen

He had no idea of time. There was only awake and sleeping or a state close to sleep where the pain dragged him into restless oblivion. Removing the handcuffs seemed like a long ago dream that fizzled into nothing. But when Tim moved his leg without the weight of the chain or the graze of the handcuffs, the dream became real. He had a feeling it had been less than a day since he'd picked the lock. Since then he'd tried to keep pushing, but hunger, pain, and exhaustion got the better of him.

I'm awake now. The last time he'd eaten or drunk was when Samantha came and he had grabbed her. Tim had expected the brother to burst through the door with fists clenched in rage. But there'd been nothing. He was free and still alive. *That had to mean something, didn't it?*

"Not if I don't get ready." He was talking to himself, cajoling his body into action. "The program only works if you work the program." A mantra he'd learned from an old friend. It seemed fitting in this setting. The road to survival could be travelled *if* he put his feet in the right furrows.

Tim reached out, his fingers travelling over the sleeping bag. The lantern was at his side, his freedom from darkness if not captivity. He flicked on the light and let out a shallow breath. Part of him didn't really believe he could escape, not weak from hunger and barely able to take a breath without a shaft of agony hobbling his every move. But he still had his mind. *Only just.* And it was his mind that he relied on now.

The lantern was cased in dark green plastic. Rigid plastic. He moved the light so it was between his legs then used both hands to twist the casing. Shivering, his fingers numb from the relentless cold, he unscrewed the outer hulk from the large globe and base. Once he had the hard plastic case off, he held it up, examining the joints. Tim smiled, his teeth like ice blocks against his lips. *It might work.*

He dashed the casing against the stone floor. The rigid plastic shattered like glass, only with a brittle crack. Scurrying forward on his knees, he gathered up the pieces, sliding the smaller bits under the sleeping bag. A few minutes later he switched off the lantern.

Listening to his own breathing, he lay awake. The waiting scared him. Not knowing when the masked man would come scared him. Disappearing into nothingness like a puff of smoke scared him. Remembering what it was like to *not* be scared steadied him. He kept his eyes open. The longer he stared into the darkness, the clearer the plan became.

He was drifting when the light came on. For a second he thought of the hospital, almost smelling the cleaning fluid and antiseptic before snapping back to reality and sitting up with a jolt. The movement set off a shiver of agony in his right side. He groaned and gritted his teeth. His broken ribs moved like shrapnel in his chest. If he punctured a lung, he'd stand no chance against the brother.

Heart pumping like an old compressor, he crouched then braced himself against the wall. Two things happened at once. The door flew open and the masked man filled the entrance. At the same moment he heard someone scream his name and his heart rate slowed. Lucy's voice was nearby and she was calling him.

Dream-like, his head shifted to the right, following his sister's voice through the stone wall. The brother turned too, as if surprised by the scream. When they faced each other again, Tim was already standing.

* * *

It was almost five o'clock when Damon pulled onto the private road. With no street lights the only illumination came from the Jeep's headlights. The twin orbs bathed the narrow slash of bitumen in cold, white light. As he approached the cul-de-sac he spotted something on the side of the road and screeched to a halt.

With the gale in full force, the dark green coat rolled off the bitumen and into the bush. Damon left the motor running and jumped out of the car. Head ducked against the wind, he jogged to keep up with the garment's movements. If he'd pulled up a minute later, the coat would have been gone.

He snagged the sleeve just as it wrapped itself around a scraggy-looking bush. The fabric felt cold and slippery on his skin. Damon stared at the coat like it was something live in his hands. Even in the wind he could smell Lucy's perfume, light and floral, on the garment.

Clenching the puffer in both hands, he walked into the headlight's arc and stood facing the house. Something had happened out on the road, something violent enough to force Lucy to drop her coat. It was then he noticed something weighty in one of the pockets.

He plunged his hand in and felt something cold and metallic. Lucy's car keys. As his fingers closed around the bunch of metal he felt something else. Damon pulled out the contents of Lucy's pocket and hissed out a breath.

Bent and creased from the weight of the keys was a photograph. Damon took in the image and his gut dropped like a deflated basketball. "Jesus, Lucy, what did you find?" His voice was hoarse and swept up by the wind.

Once more his gaze went back to the house. There were no lights, just the partial moonlight over the roof. Lucy had described the house, but seeing it like this, painted inky blue against the night sky, Damon felt a jab of foreboding.

Still holding the coat, he jammed the photo and keys in his pocket and raced back to the Jeep. The coat couldn't have been on the road long or the wind would have taken it. Whatever took place must have occurred no more than ten or fifteen minutes ago. He tossed Lucy's coat on the passenger seat and turned off the engine, watching the road disappear into almost total darkness. Once he had his phone, he reached under the seat and pulled out the gun. He removed it from the black bag and climbed out of the Jeep, wedging the firearm into the back of his jeans.

Without any real hope of her answering, he swiped at the sheen of sweat gathering on his forehead and called Lucy's phone one last time. He listened to the ringing and paced back and forth on the road, the weight of the gun pressing into his lower back. Five rings and he was ready to disconnect when something caught his attention and the muscles in his shoulders tensed. The faint sound was almost swamped by the wind, but he recognised it. Somewhere nearby a phone was ringing.

Damon stopped moving and cocked his head, listening. The ringing was intermittent, audible during strong gusts and then gone with the lull. He disconnected before the call went to voicemail and rang again. This time he turned on the light in his phone and swept the edge of the road until the glare landed on tyre marks leading into the bush.

His blood was pumping now, a surge of heat building in his muscles. Tyre marks cut through a narrow clearing, ploughing over small bushes and bending back rangy limbs. Damon followed the path using the phone light that moved in jerky time with his steps. Within thirty seconds the light bounced off the back of the Saab.

He wasn't sure what he'd been expecting, but seeing Lucy's car dark and half buried in the bush was almost like coming across a tomb. As he approached he pulled Lucy's keys from his pocket and clicked the lock. The car sprang to life with a *bleep*. Orange lights painted the surrounding scrub with an eerie glow.

Damon hesitated. He'd seen things while on deployment, things that had never left him. Things that made him wonder if there was enough good left in the world to make evil worth fighting. But staring at Lucy's car, he didn't think he could bring himself to look inside. Suddenly every horror he'd ever encountered wasn't enough to prepare him if she was inside that car or if he was too late.

The last metre or so was the longest. He reached the vehicle and stopped at the boot. The wind twisted through the trees, their branches tapping and scraping on the vehicle like spectral fingers. Hand shaking on the latch, he closed his eyes for a fraction of a second then flung up the lid. Lucy's smoky green eyes, now frozen and cloudy, stared back at him. He shook his head and the image vanished. Iron grey carpet, a few spots of sand, an umbrella, but otherwise empty.

Damon tilted his head back and caught sight of the moon, its cold surface watching him like a milky eye. He still had to search the interior. A spinning wheel of images turned in his mind: Lucy crumpled on the back seat or slumped over the wheel, her face half-covered with a curtain of soft brown hair. *Just get it over with*. He slammed the boot and moved to the driver's side.

The back seat was clear. He clenched his teeth and moved on. Pushing a clump of scraggy bush aside and turning side on, Damon managed to reach the driver's window. Leaning his hand on the icy glass, he surveyed the empty seat. Lucy's handbag sat on the passenger side floor.

Like the discarded coat, the mundane items took on a sinister significance when abandoned.

There was nothing more to be learned from the car, so Damon locked the vehicle and headed back to the cul-de-sac. Almost at the road he heard the rumble of an engine and slowed his pace. Still partially hidden by bush, he edged closer to the bitumen.

Headlights lit up the Jeep. A door thudded and Damon heard the scuff of shoes on the unsealed road. He moved closer to the road and caught sight of a figure dressed in dark pants and jacket, tall and muscular in the wash of the lights. Damon scanned the area. Unless there was someone in the car, the man was alone.

Damon pushed back his jacket and touched his fingers to the grip of the gun. As he stepped out of the bush he let his hand hang at his side loose and ready to reach around and take hold of the fire arm.

"Damon?" The man's voice carried a familiar edge of tension.

Damon's shoulders, bunched with stiffness, relaxed. He nodded and walked towards the UCO. "What took you so long?"

* * *

The pain was white hot, a jolt of searing heat convulsing her muscles. Lucy hit the ground, writhing, mouth open and neck straining in a soundless scream. Almost as suddenly as the jab from the cattle prod brought the agony, her muscles relaxed and the pain fizzled, leaving her panting and staring at the sky.

"Up." Ruth's voice, like gravel on fine china, pulled Lucy back to the moment.

The smell of cigarettes and damp grass clogged her nose as the woman's face hovered over her. Lucy thought of refusing to move. Letting her head loll in the dirt and grass, she managed to focus on the woman's voice. Ruth held the prod close to Lucy's face. "Move or the next one's on your neck."

The thought of another jolt, the scalding heat and excruciating pulse twisting her nerves, got her moving. Lucy rolled onto her stomach and pulled herself into a clumsy crouch, her muscles trembling with weakness. It took all her strength, but she managed to get her legs working and she was able to stand.

Ruth waved the cattle prod, motioning for Lucy to enter the house. Again the idea of running came and went. Her legs were still numb, barely responding to the signals from her brain.

"Come on." Ruth planted a hand on Lucy's back and shoved her. The woman's bony arms were stronger than they looked or maybe Lucy was still off balance. The push sent Lucy tipping forward. The ground came into view again but the world righted itself as Lucy grabbed the doorframe.

Inside the old building the walls were a silt-coloured network of misshaped natural stone. The floor, covered in some sort of red linoleum, reminded Lucy of a long, hungry tongue that stretched the length of the building with rooms running off it right and left. A blast of stagnant air, putrid and gaseous, rolled over her, rocking her stomach with nausea.

Barely over the doorstep, she saw a figure emerge from an open doorway. Taking in the man's bare upper body and grotesque rubber mask, Lucy stuttered out a yelp. In her panic she tried to back pedal out of the house, but Ruth was behind her, blocking any escape. The building was a nightmare of horrifying smells and images, pulling Lucy down into near hysteria.

She was close to breaking. Her body screamed with pain and fatigue and her mind ricocheted from the man to the object clutched in his meaty fist: a loop of wire, crusty with brownish stains. *This is madness.* This constant twisting of fear and horror. *They're going to kill me, but I'll be insane by then, so it might not matter.*

"Go on," Ruth said to the man.

Lucy recognised the navy pants and thick build. Holsey was wearing an old-lady mask. She slumped against the doorframe, not bothering to suppress a sob.

"Make it quick with him so we can get the two of them downstairs." Ruth then spoke over Lucy's shoulder. "I'll keep an eye on our friend here."

Holsey stood for a second, his pale eyes shiny and glazed through the holes in the thick rubber. His free hand clenched and unclenched, the gesture menacing and oddly mechanical. In spite of the fear, it occurred to Lucy that maybe Samson wasn't the only one in the family with a fragmented identity. The image of the ramshackle garden, with its rotting play equipment, flashed in her mind. She held her breath until Holsey turned away and walked down the hall.

With the return of coherent thought, Lucy felt a measure of control returning. She watched Holsey stop at a door and slide back the bolt. "I told my producer I was visiting Samson. He's sending a news crew in the morning." She hoped her tone sounded less panicky than she felt. "There's no way out of this for you." She turned and searched Ruth's face, hoping to see some sign of nervousness.

"Shut up." The woman's mouth pursed; deep gouges fanned her lips, etched into the skin from years of heavy smoking. It gave Lucy an idea.

"Can I have a cigarette?"

Ruth blinked and dragged her gaze off Holsey. "No, but you can watch me have one." She tucked the cattle prod under her arm and reached into her coat pocket.

Holsey opened the door and stepped inside the room. Ruth was saying something, but Lucy's attention was flicking back and forth between the woman's hollow cheeks and Holsey's shirtless frame. The roaring of her blood pulsed in Lucy's ears almost blocking the sound of Ruth's voice. There was no more time. Tim was in that room and any second now Holsey would use that piece of bloodstained wire to end her brother's life.

Lucy let her hand brush her hip, feeling the pen she'd snatched from Holsey's console. With nothing else at hand it would have to do. She dipped her fingers into the pocket and slipped out the pen. Ruth's red head was bent over the lighter, sucking in smoke.

Sounds of movement came from down the hall. A grunt like a blow was landed. Before Ruth's head could rise from the lighter, Lucy plunged the point of the pen into the woman's ear, gasping at the crunching pop that followed. Ruth wailed out a scream that bounced off the stone walls like a siren, shrill and agonised. Blood, dark and warm, flooded over Lucy's hand and splattered the linoleum. Gagging at the globby mess, Lucy pushed the woman away.

Seeming to be responding to Ruth's cry, Holsey appeared in the hallway. Ruth dropped the cattle prod and clawed at her ear, her eyes bulging and rolling wildly as she reeled sideways and blood ran between her splayed fingers. Lucy stooped and grabbed the cattle prod. Eyes on Holsey and bracing for an attack, she held the brown baton-shaped weapon in front of her, arms shuddering as adrenalin surged through her body.

"Gordon. Gordon, do something." Ruth's voice was a croak filled with pain.

But Holsey only staggered and clutched his shoulder as blood dripped through his hands and ran down his bulging gut. It was then that Lucy noticed something lodged in the man's shoulder, buried between the edge of the rubber mask and the tendons. At the left of Holsey's neck was a jagged shaft of something dark and shiny under the light.

"Oh shit." The words came out around laboured gasps. Lucy tried to keep the prod up in front of her, but the blood on her hands made the weapon slick and almost impossible to grip.

The red linoleum around Holsey's shoes was turning dark under the volume of blood. He stumbled left and slumped against the wall. Lucy's hair was plastered to her face in sweaty clumps as she struggled to hold the prod and keep her eyes on Holsey.

"T...Tim." She managed to get the name past her lips, but the sound was little more than a whisper. "Tim!" This time she cried out her brother's name through a blur of tears.

"You bitch." Ruth was sitting on the floor, rocking back and forth, her head cradled in her hands.

He stumbled into the hallway, a patchwork of dirt and bruising covering his upper body. Blinking in the scene, Tim's face turned in Lucy's direction. He limped towards her, barely glancing as Holsey slid down the wall and sat hard on his ass.

"Lucy?" Tim's swollen lips moved as his pace increased.

Lucy let the cattle prod hang at her side. He was alive. Her legs wobbled but she managed to stay standing. Even battered and swollen she knew his face. Something inside her fluttered with a mixture of joy and relief. She rubbed the heel of her bloody hand across her cheek, smudging blood and tears over her face. Out of the corner of her eye she caught sight of something yellow. A blur of colour and then Samantha was in front of her, arm raised, and rushing at Tim.

Lucy raised the prod and swung at Nightmesser's moving back, but her reaction time was too slow. The prod scraped Samantha's back, barely glancing off her blouse. She heard Tim say something, but couldn't recognise the words, only the shock in his voice.

The knife, large and highly polished, reflected a dazzling glint of light as it came down on Tim. Lucy screamed, her cries matching Samantha's raging shriek.

Lucy heard the knife whistling through the air and then Tim's voice. She ran towards them, not sure if it was Tim calling her name that got her moving or the cruel realisation that if she didn't stop Nightmesser and the zig-zagging blade she'd lose her brother just when she almost had him back.

* * *

There was no sound from inside Nightmesser's house. Damon walked from the side door to the rear. He looked up but couldn't see any lights. The building had a flat, empty feel of a place left to decay for years.

"He's not here." Brock rounded the curved wall and joined Damon at the back of the house.

"This place is huge. He could be inside and not answering." Damon turned and stared out into the darkness of the garden, the glow from his torch picking out a child's slide, rusty and dilapidated. "Lucy's coat couldn't have been on the road long, not in this wind. And I didn't see any car leaving the private road." He turned to Brock. "We could probably get in through one of the glass doors. It might be worth taking a look around."

Brock stood with his hands on his hips, appearing to be studying the curved gravel driveway. "What about that?" He nodded into the darkness.

Damon followed Brock's gaze and spotted the dark outline of another structure. "Is that a garage?"

Brock nodded. "Let's see if the car's here."

The terrace was raised, sitting a metre and a half above the driveway. Not wasting time with the stairs, Damon jumped from the terrace to the driveway, landing with a crunch on the gravel. A second later Brock joined him and pulled out his phone. Adding his light to Damon's, they walked towards the garage.

The triple garage was also in darkness. Brock bent and caught hold of the door, rattling the lock. Surprisingly, the garage was unlocked and the door tilted upwards with a tired squeak.

The space to the right was dominated by a cream-coloured Mercedes, an early Seventies soft-top in almost perfect condition. The air inside the garage was musty, a combination of damp and decay. Damon shone the light on the wall to the left of the door and spotted a light switch. With the light on, the contents of the garage was revealed: stacks of boxes, a jumble of broken furniture, and shelves of dusty crockery.

"Jesus." Damon ran his hand over the back of his neck and his palm came away damp with sweat. "It looks like half the house is stuffed in here."

Brock pointed to the Mercedes. "I've seen Nightmesser driving that around town. It's the only car registered under his name so I'd say he didn't drive away."

Damon stepped out of the garage, grateful for the cold wind on his face. Time was spinning out of control. With every minute they wasted, the chances of finding Lucy were slipping away. Nightmesser hadn't driven away, at least not in his Mercedes. Their only option now pointed to breaking in and searching the giant house. If the house was anything like the garage, it could take up to an hour. *Longer if we're looking for a body*. His gut clenched at the idea.

He accepted that Aidan was dead. As much as it hurt, Damon was a realist and he couldn't convince himself that the young man he'd served with was miraculously alive after going missing six months ago. When Lucy told him about Tim, he'd half made up his mind that her brother was dead too, even after less than a week. But Lucy had been gone for less than an hour. He wouldn't give up on her, not until he tore the house apart and searched every building and acre of bush associated with the Nightmesser name.

"Okay. Let's search the house." Brock turned off the light, casting them back into darkness.

Damon dragged his attention away from the house and watched as Brock pulled the tilt-door down. When the garage was secure, Damon turned on his light. The glare fell on the bushland to the right of the garage. As he moved to follow Brock back to the terrace, something caught his attention and his heart rate jumped up a notch. Probably easier to spot in daylight, under the cover of night the track had remained hidden until the phone light shined directly on it.

"Brock." Damon's voice was loud in the darkness. "I've found something."

They travelled in Damon's Jeep, only because it was closest to Nightmesser's driveway. As they bumped along the uneven track Damon felt tension like a hungry animal chewing at his nerves. He glanced at Brock, noticing the man's calm posture and felt a stab of irritation.

"If you knew about the plantation, why have you been sitting on your hands waiting? Why not shut the thing down and arrest everyone?" Damon's eyes were travelling between the track and Brock's impassive face. "I only ask because waiting probably cost lives."

Brock kept his eyes on the dirt road. "Two months before I arrived in Night Town, the Senior Sergeant here, a guy named Robert Ackerman, shot himself in the head." Brock's voice was flat, almost emotionless. "Ackerman had been the senior officer in Night Town for almost five years."

"You think he was involved with Nightmesser and the plantation?" Damon decreased his speed as they rounded a sharp bend.

Brock jerked his chin at the track. "Watch out."

Damon jammed his foot on the brake just as a roo bounced onto the soft sandy track. Both men jolted forward and then back. As he hit the seat, the gun dug into the small of Damon's back. "Fuck." He let the word out around a long breath.

The large marsupial's ears twitched as it surveyed the car with curious dark eyes before bounding into the bush. Still breathing hard, Damon continued driving.

"Yeah, but with Ackerman dead, an opportunity arose and I was brought in." Brock continued, seemingly unfazed by the close encounter with the kangaroo. "But Nightmesser was never really important. My target was a woman. Ruth Holsey, at least that's the name she's using now."

Damon shook his head. "Holsey?"

"Yep. As far as we know, Gordon Holsey met Ruth Marsh when he was stationed in the Goldfields. She was running a large brothel. Ruth was well known for being hard on the girls; quick with her hands. She was questioned in connection with an unsolved murder in 2008, a young male prostitute beaten then strangled in a home invasion." He let out a sigh. "No charges were ever brought, but when Holsey returned to Night Town six years earlier, Ruth came with him."

"So why wait?" Damon steered the car around a dip and then spun the wheel, straightening up. "If this woman Ruth Holsey's in town and involved in the plantation isn't that enough?"

"Ruth has contacts. People much further up the chain. That was what I was waiting for. But..." he trailed off.

"But now that's all fucked up?" Damon finished for him.

Brock shrugged and changed the subject. "Have you got a license for that gun?"

In spite of everything Damon couldn't help smiling. "What gun?"

He thought he saw Brock's mouth twitch. Maybe it was the shadows thrown by the car's dim interior or maybe that's what passed for a smile from the UCO.

The Jeep bounced over a hump in the road and Damon caught sight of a hulking shape and the distinctive glow of lights, sharp and unnatural in the faint moonlight.

"There's a building." Damon pointed over the steering wheel.

The tension that had been building in his muscles intensified until his fingers turned white on the steering wheel. As they coasted the last thirty metres Damon spotted two vehicles parked ahead of a dark building and an open door that spilled light onto the scene.

"Holsey's here." Brock's hand was on the door. "That dark four-wheel-drive is Ruth's."

Damon stopped short of the police car and turned off the engine, flinging open the door while the vehicle still shuddered. With one foot out of the Jeep, a scream — jagged and unmistakably terrified — fractured the night. Damon left the car door open and ran, pulling the gun from his jeans as he shouldered past Brock.

The wind had dropped. The threatening storm now dwindled to a breeze as Damon flicked off the safety and charged the building. There were voices, a cacophony of screams and cries.

"Wait." He heard Brock caution behind him, but didn't stop. He reached the doorway and ducked to the right, holding the gun down and in both hands. He made himself count to three, slowing his heart rate and steadying his hands before craning his neck and looking into the building.

The scene inside was confusion, a bloody nightmarish tableau of violence. For a heartbeat Damon was frozen and then his thoughts cleared and he raised the gun.

Chapter Seventeen

Movement was nightmarishly slow, like the red linoleum was a swampy mouth, pulling her down, and slowing her progress. She could see Nightmesser's back, the blonde locks bouncing as his arm rose and fell, and Tim trying to ward off the blade, his forearms held high like a fleshy shield.

Lucy's legs were buckling, her vision shrouded by dark spots, but she held onto the prod and somehow managed to keep moving. Someone was calling her name. The voice broke through her panic, puncturing the fuzz that clouded her mind.

"Lucy, duck." She recognised the voice, the smooth sonorous tone, but the words were a jumble. "Duck, Lucy. Duck!"

Tim was on one knee now, the flesh on his forearm flapping like a meaty tongue as Nightmesser loomed over him with the knife raised. And suddenly the words made sense.

Lucy dropped to the floor, her knees smacking the linoleum, the cattle prod rolling out of her grasp. A thunderous crack filled the hallway and burst in her ears like an explosion. Nightmesser crumpled, landing hard as if his legs had been kicked out from under him.

The air, still putrid with the smell of human waste, was now laced with a mixture of smoke and blood. Lucy turned and saw Damon with his arms out and a gun still levelled in her direction. When his gaze found hers, he lowered the gun. He moved to run to her but someone was at his elbow. With the gun shot still resounding in her ears, Lucy saw Damon hand the gun to Brock. Her mind, reeling with shock, couldn't process what was happening. Why was Brock with Damon? Instead she turned away and crawled towards her brother.

Before she reached Tim, Damon's arms circled her, lifting and supporting her as they made their way towards her brother.

"Tim?" Lucy's voice was hoarse from screaming. "Tim, it's me."

He was on the floor, arms in his lap with blood pooling around his legs. Beside her, Damon stripped off his jumper and wrapped it around Tim's bleeding arm.

"Ambulance and a helicopter's on the way," Brock called from the doorway.

Tim's eyes were closed. One was so swollen she doubted he could open it. Damon took Tim's shoulders and lowered him to the floor. As he moved her brother, Lucy heard Damon speaking to him, explaining that the ambulance was coming.

Behind her, Ruth was swearing then crying. At one point she heard Brock's voice, cold and unemotional, telling the woman to shut up. Nightmesser's body was slumped to Tim's right. Lucy tried not to let her eyes wander to the dead man, but as Damon rolled Tim into the recovery position, she found her gaze landing on Samson.

The blonde wig had tipped back, revealing the man's thinning hair. His pale eyes were wide, staring vacantly in her direction. There were splatters of blood on his white blouse. *Tim's blood.* Nightmesser was a twisted man. Mentally ill, maybe incapable of stopping himself from doing unspeakable things, but as she tore her eyes off the dead man she felt no pity, only loathing.

With Tim on his side, Lucy touched his face and was surprised by the coldness of his skin. "Tim. It's Lucy. You're safe now." Tears were running down her cheeks. "Can you hear me?"

One of Tim's eyes opened and his lips moved. Lucy lowered her head until her ear was almost touching his cracked and bloody lips. "Sorry about your b...birthday."

* * *

She woke with a start. For a few seconds Lucy had absolutely no idea where she was. It was only the smell of antiseptic and the rails on the bed that grounded her thoughts and she remembered. The ambulance ride to the tiny hospital in Margaret River had been an eternity over the bumpy track as the vehicle raced through the night.

Turning her head set off a throbbing ache in her skull. Like angry fingers, the pain gripped her forehead in an unflinching clench. Moving not only hurt, it set off waves of nausea, and saliva flooded her mouth.

Keeping her head still and rolling her eyes, she was able to look to the left where Damon slept with his arms crossed over his stomach and chin resting on his chest. The plastic hospital chair barely contained his large body. Just watching his precarious balance made her already sore neck stiffen.

Enjoying the semi-silence of the hospital room, Lucy watched Damon sleep. Hair messy and flattened on one side and day-old stubble darkening his chin and cheeks, he looked very much as he had that first day on the road. The day she found him. Or had he found her? It didn't really matter. They'd found each other and for the first time in weeks she felt warm.

His eyes opened like he'd sensed her watching him. "How's the head?" His voice was thick with fatigue. She wondered how long it had been since he had slept.

"Not too bad." She managed a smile, the small movement enough to make her scalp burn. "You look beat. You should go and get some sleep."

He straightened up in the chair and nodded. "I will. Just wanted to let you know Tim's been taken to Royal Perth Hospital. They're going to operate on his arm."

"Thank you." Her eyes were heavy. It felt like her body wanted to shut down and draw in on itself and retreat from the world.

Damon's whiskey-coloured eyes looked softer in the gloomy morning light that slipped through a small gap in the curtains. "No problem. Just wanted you to know where he was."

"No. Thank you for everything you've done for me... For Tim. For what you did last night and, you know..." She was having trouble expressing herself. Her mind kept drawing a blank, the words slipping away before she could catch them.

He leaned forward in the chair and put his hand on hers, his skin warm and comforting. "No thanks needed. Just feel better." He stood and leaned over her. For a second she thought he meant to kiss her on the lips and her heart fluttered, but his stubbly chin grazed her forehead and his warm lips touched her head.

"I'll be back this afternoon with coffee." He turned to leave.

"Wait." Her voice was stronger now, sounding more natural. "Aidan?"

A slight shake of his head, an almost imperceptible movement, but somehow full of regret. "I'll fill you in when I get back." And with that he was gone.

Alone in the small room, Lucy closed her eyes to images from the night before: blood and screams. Her screams tried to work their way to the forefront of her mind. There was so much to process. So many horrors to reconcile that she doubted sleep would come. But her depleted mind and body quickly swept her into a deep slumber.

* * *

It was early afternoon when she woke to the sound of rattling wheels and the whoosh of the door. A nurse, young and fresh-faced, checked her vitals, chatting in an overly cheerful voice about the prospect of rain.

"When will the doctor be around?" Lucy didn't mean to be rude, but cutting the young woman off seemed to be her only option.

"Hmm." Her name badge identified her as Carrie. "He'll be in sometime in the next hour." She made a clicking sound with her tongue. "There are only fifty beds in this hospital, but there's never enough time to get everything done. I started at eight this morning and I—"

"Sorry." Lucy pulled herself up in bed. The pain in her head had diminished to a sullen throb. "My brother's in Royal Perth. He's having surgery today and I really need to be there." She touched the neckline of the washed-out blue hospital gown. "Where are my clothes?"

The young nurse frowned and her voice changed from cheerful to business-like. "You have a concussion." She ran her hand over the blankets, smoothing a non-existent wrinkle. "I'd say the doctor will want you to spend the night just to be sure." She seemed about to say more but hesitated.

"What? Is it my brother?" Lucy's chest tightened and as her pulse jumped, so did the throbbing in her skull. "Has something happened?" She was leaning forward, fighting a burst of nausea and ready to fling back the blankets.

"No. No, no. Nothing like that." Carrie held up her hand with her palm open and stiff, a gesture for Lucy to stop moving. "It's just... Well, the police want to speak to you once you've seen the doctor."

"Oh." Lucy leaned back. "Yes, of course."

With so much to process she hadn't had time to think about the police, but it made sense there'd be questions, not to mention her statement to make. An image jumped into her mind of Damon handing the gun to Brock. The memory was vague and overshadowed by the image of Nightmesser lying on the floor with his wig askew and his dead eyes rolled in her direction. But with the police eager to speak to her, she suddenly felt unsure of what she should tell them about the shooting.

Damon had saved her brother's life. If he hadn't shot Samson, Lucy had no doubt the man would have killed Tim. Maybe her, too. But would the police see it that way? Until he fired the shot, Lucy had no idea Damon even had a gun.

Carrie pulled the curtains, letting sunlight flood the gloomy room. Lucy tried to think, struggling to put her words in order. "I... um. My friend is coming in this afternoon." The nurse stopped fussing with the curtains and began pouring Lucy a glass of water, her expression guarded. "I'd like to speak to him first." She forced a weak smile. "He'll be able to give me an update on my brother and..." She was reaching for something solid, a reason to see Damon before the police. "I don't think I can concentrate until I know he's okay." Her voice shook. It wasn't a lie. She really did need to know how Tim was doing. "Sorry." Lucy swiped at her eyes. "I'm too emotional to handle all this."

The nurse's face relaxed into concern. "You poor thing. I'll make sure your friend gets in after the doctor comes." She clamped her lips together. "I don't know much about what happened to you, but you've been through a lot. You just relax. Lunch will be here soon." She handed Lucy the glass of water she'd been pouring. She didn't remember asking for a drink, but took the glass and drank. "That's better," Carrie continued. "After you've eaten, I'll help you to have a shower." The nurse's eyes were brown, a warm chocolate colour, kind eyes that revealed genuine concern. Lucy felt a stab of guilt for manipulating the woman. "A nice hot shower and you'll feel much better."

Lucy gave the nurse a grateful smile. "Thank you."

Lunch was a tuna salad and a cup of vanilla custard which Lucy devoured like a hungry tiger. With food in her stomach, the nausea abated, and as promised a hot shower did help her feel more like herself.

At around three o'clock Damon appeared in the doorway, balancing a cardboard tray with two coffees and pulling her little red suitcase. The brightly coloured valise looked oddly comical in Damon's hand and Lucy couldn't help smiling.

"You look better." He set the coffee down on the bed tray and parked the suitcase near the locker next to the bed.

Lucy picked up one of the coffees and took a sip, savouring the warm rich flavour. "This is just what I needed." She paused, inhaling the strong, sweet aroma. "Thanks. And thanks for bringing my stuff."

He pulled the chair close to the bed and sat. "It's the least I can do." He raised his eyebrows. "The nurse said you were desperate to see me. Emotional even." His smile, slightly crooked, looked like it was holding back a chuckle.

Lucy laughed and uncharacteristically blushed at the same time, wincing at the pain that prickled her scalp. "Don't make me laugh. It hurts my head." But in spite of the soreness, it felt good to laugh again. "I had to say something." She spoke around another sip of coffee. "The police want to talk to me and…" She set the cup down. "I didn't know what to tell them about the gun."

Damon shrugged. "It must have been Nightmesser's or Holsey's. I found it on the table in that weird kitchen to the right of the entrance." As he spoke Lucy had the feeling he was giving her a version of the truth, a version he would tell the police.

She let out a breath and leaned her head back on the pillows. "Yes. That's what I thought." For a moment neither spoke. It felt like mentioning Nightmesser's name pulled them both back into the nightmarish memory.

Damon was first to break the silence. "The police are being pretty tight-lipped with what they've uncovered in Nightmesser's house and the old building where you found Tim." He ran a hand over the back of his neck. "I've been on the phone with Aidan's mother. Even after six months she was still hoping..."

He didn't have to say any more. Lucy was all too familiar with that constant hope, the way it curled itself up in your brain; the need to feed it and keep the doubt at bay. The way it ate at your soul until every moment was a see-saw of faith and uncertainty.

"What about Holsey and Ruth?" Surprisingly, she hadn't given the two much thought since leaving the hellish old building.

Damon took a sip of his coffee before answering. "They're both at Royal Perth."

"In the same hospital as Tim?" Lucy couldn't believe what she was hearing. After everything those monsters had put her brother through, they were still allowed to breathe the same air. A spark of anger burned in her chest. Anger at the police. Anger at a system that was indifferent to men like Tim and Aidan, seeing them as lesser beings because, for whatever reasons, they were unable to function as normal, whatever that meant.

He spread his hands in a *what are you gonna do* gesture. "They're under guard. Brock mentioned a bedside hearing to lay some preliminary charges, pending what's uncovered in the house."

"Brock?" Lucy remembered seeing him the night before but had no idea how he came to be with Damon at the old building.

Damon put his cup on the bed trolley. "There's a lot I need to tell you."

Damon talked for almost half an hour, only stopping to sip his coffee and answer Lucy's questions. When he was finished she was astounded that the police were willing to spend money and manpower on an operation to uncover a drug syndicate, but at no time did they realise there was something even more sinister going on in the town.

"So, what now?" Lucy asked. "Do you think it will come out that the cops had no real idea what was going on in Night Town?"

"Not if they can help it." Damon's tone was flat, resigned. "These things have a way of being hushed up. My guess is a press conference tomorrow. An opportunity for the Commissioner to put enough spin on the story so the cops come off sounding like heroes."

Lucy thought for a moment. "Is my laptop in the suitcase?"

Damon nodded and picked up the case. "What are you planning?" he asked over his shoulder as he set the valise on the end of the bed and opened it.

Lucy leaned forward, rubbing at her aching head. "When I talk to the police, I'm sure they'll warn me not to go public with anything that could jeopardise their case against Holsey and Ruth. But..." she drew the word out. "There's nothing to stop me giving my producer a few carefully worded questions to toss out at the press conference."

Damon set the laptop up on the trolley. As he bent to plug the device into the nearest outlet, a nurse appeared at the door. Not Carrie, but an older woman Lucy didn't recognise.

"Sorry to interrupt." The woman didn't sound sorry as her eyes moved between Lucy and Damon, scanning the trolley as if expecting to catch them passing contraband. "There are two polices officers waiting to see you. I'll send them in," she continued, without giving Lucy a chance to argue.

"I'd better go. I'm supposed to report to the local police to give a statement at four o'clock." Damon picked up the empty cups and tossed them in the bin near the bathroom. "I'll come back in the morning. If they decide you're fit to leave, I'll drive you back to Perth." He stood with his hands on his hips.

Lucy felt a quiver of nervousness at the prospect of rehashing the dreadful details of the previous night. Part of her wasn't really ready to admit some of the things that had happened. Not to herself, let alone to two cops she'd never met. She wished Damon could stay. She almost said as much, but stopped herself. He'd done so much already. She couldn't keep pushing for more. In a day or so he'd probably disappear from her life. It would be crazy to start relying on him now.

"Are you sure?" She pushed her hair back and pulled the blankets up, not sure why she was starting to fidget. "I mean about the lift… It's a long drive."

"Yeah, I'm sure." He raised a hand in a sort of half-wave. "See you in the morning." He left. This time without kissing her.

Almost as soon as he disappeared around the door, the two officers entered. Lucy wondered if they'd been standing directly outside listening. Maybe she was being paranoid, but after the events of the last week *and* discovering Holsey, a senior constable, was involved in not only drugs, but murder, she thought she had a right to be cautious. She closed the laptop and braced herself for what she knew would be a difficult interview.

The two male detectives were surprisingly gentle with their questions. While she was relieved that they didn't grill her, she couldn't help wondering if they'd been told to go easy on her because of her job as a journalist and her knowledge of the police force's shortcomings in this case. Either way she was glad it was over, for now.

With the questions over she allowed herself a few minutes before emailing Matt about the possibility of a press conference. In those minutes she lay back on the pillows. At first she struggled with the desire for a cigarette. Today would be the first time in over a year she'd gone a full day without smoking.

Picking at the edge of the sheet, she tried to tell herself that after coming close to losing her life she'd never smoke again. But there was a more cynical side to her that knew real life didn't work like that. As much as her body was craving nicotine she also wanted to see Damon. In just a few days he'd started to become... Her thoughts stuttered to a halt. *What has he become?* She didn't know how to answer her own question.

Would they say goodbye tomorrow and end up sending each other a few text messages? Followed by the inevitable fading of the commitment to stay in touch? She rubbed her left temple with her fingertips, trying to massage away the ache. But the pain went deeper than the concussion. Picturing herself back in her family home, with nothing but memories surrounding her was like a physical ache. An ache made worse after a brief glimpse of how different her life could be.

This isn't me. She wasn't a woman to moon and pine over a man. She pulled herself up in the bed, wincing at the stab of pain in her skull. She opened the laptop and did what she'd always done when the world seemed an uncertain place. She threw herself into work.

* * *

Damon arrived at eight the next morning. Lucy rose at seven a.m. and had showered and washed her hair before breakfast. When he entered the room she was fully dressed and watching the morning news.

By way of greeting he held up a cardboard tray with two coffees. "Looks like you're ready to go." He put the coffees down on the bed trolley. "What did the doctor say?"

Lucy picked up a cup and sat cross-legged on the unmade bed. "Thanks for this." She took a sip and nodded. "Nice." She grabbed the remote and muted the television before continuing. "The doctor hasn't said anything yet. He's supposed to be coming around any minute now. But..." She jerked her shoulders. "I'm going either way."

Damon raised his eyebrows. "That bad here?"

Looking into his eyes, she had the urge to blurt out her feelings and ask him if this was something. Something she wanted it to be or if they were just friends. Instead, she sipped her coffee.

"No. It's okay here. They've all been nice, but I spoke to Tim last night." She fidgeted with the edge of the sheet. "He was groggy. He said the operation went well, but he sounded... I don't know, shell-shocked is probably what it was."

"That's understandable under the circumstances." Maybe it was her imagination, but Damon seemed to be studying her, watching her fingers as they plucked at the bedding. "He's been through hell. It's bound to be tough."

"Yes. I know, you're right, but I think he needs me there." She forced a smile. "If the offer of a lift is still on the table that is?"

"Yep." He picked up his cup. "I'm ready whenever you are." But before he could put the coffee to his lips, something on the screen caught his attention. "Lucy, put the sound up."

Lucy's vision narrowed until all she could see was the television. Nightmesser's house, gothic and ominous, filled the TV screen. There was yellow crime scene tape ringing the driveway entrance and a cluster of white vehicles and police cars blocking the cul-de-sac. She hit the sound button and the female news reader's voice filled the small hospital room.

The house is now a crime scene with police and forensic officers combing the property. The local limestone quarry has been closed and a team of police, including canine units, are reported to be sweeping the area.

The image cut to an aerial shot of the house and surrounding bush. The shot landed on the building where Tim had been kept. The steep black roof of the old building looked stark, like a scar across the lush green of the forest. To the rear of the building a broad white forensic tent abutted the stone wall. Seeing the building even on the television screen was like being dumped back in the moment she'd watched her brother slashed and stabbed by Nightmesser. She could almost hear the sound the blade made as it whistled through the air, and the sickening sight of flesh being torn open.

Lucy put a hand to her chest, trying to steady her breathing as the reporter's voice continued to catalogue the grim discoveries on Nightmesser's property.

So far officers have removed seven industrial-sized plastic barrels believed to contain human remains. As yet, no victims have been named, but the commissioner is expected to give a press conference sometime this morning.

"Lucy." Damon's hand was on her shoulder. "Are you okay?" He took the remote from her clammy fingers and clicked off the TV. "Here." He poured her a glass of water and pushed it into her hand.

She took a sip and drew a long breath, her lungs beginning to work again. She'd never had a full-blown panic attack but suspected the strangled feeling of being unable to catch her breath while her skin burned with fear was close.

"I'm okay." She managed to get the words out as her breathing returned to normal. "I just couldn't catch my breath that's all."

Damon sat back down. "You've been through hell. It's going to take you and Tim a while to come to grips with everything. Just seeing that place gives me the fucking creeps."

Lucy couldn't hold in a shaky chuckle. He wasn't like anyone she'd ever met. Instead of platitudes or vague promises that everything would be all right, Damon didn't dress things up. "I like the way you always say it like it is." She put the glass back on the bed trolley and stood. "I'm going to find a doctor or a nurse, maybe even the janitor and tell them I'm leaving."

Damon nodded. "Good idea. Let's put some space between us and Night Town."

Twenty minutes later they were in Damon's Jeep, heading back to Perth. Lucy put the window down and let the fresh morning air wash over her face. It felt good to be leaving. Better than good. It was like throwing off a heavy weight and stepping into the sun.

"Lucy." Damon's voice was sombre, shaking her out of her reverie with a jolt. Never at a loss for words, she found herself unable to speak. "I think we need to talk."

Chapter Eighteen

A field of pink flowers, nameless beauties that appeared almost overnight, swayed in the late spring sun as the afternoon light painted the surrounding trees gold. It had been three days since Lucy had last seen Tim. Like the spring sunlight, he came and went without much fuss. She worried less these days. Sometimes she'd go almost twenty-four hours without thinking about Night Town. But there were times like last night. Times she'd wake in a bath of sweat alone and terrified, still hearing the blade land and the screams tear at her soul.

She closed the laptop, rubbed her eyes, and then pinched the bridge of her nose between her fingers. It was almost five months since the horror of Night Town. Something had died in her that night, leaving her incapable of crime reporting, incapable of compartmentalising her personal life from a profession where death and misery was something to be detailed and proffered to the world.

Now sitting on the veranda of her new home with acres of bush and wildlife on her doorstep, she was content to work on human interest pieces, stories of battlers who beat the odds. The sort of research and writing she would have scoffed at not so long ago now seemed a more gentle contribution to the world. She'd even been considering writing a novel.

She pushed back from the table and grabbed the pair of battered trainers she kept next to the back door. She needed to walk, get her head in the right space before opening the email. She tossed her flip-flops under the table and pulled on the trainers, an odd combination with her light cotton sundress. One of the advantages of living on a big property and working mostly from home was being able to wear whatever she wanted and not give a damn.

As she padded down the back steps, a sound caught her attention and she tipped her head to the left, listening. In the distance a dog barked, a playful sound that eased her nerves. Tim was somewhere close by with Atlas, the rescue dog they brought home soon after moving into the new house. The two-year-old shepherd mix stuck to Tim like glue. It was like the stray recognised a parallel soul in her brother and the two were now inseparable.

Lucy had no idea how long Tim would be content to wander the property before growing restless and disappearing to some distant beach or forest. But she'd made a home for them, a place where they could build new memories and, in time, heal. Winding her hair into a lose plait, she headed towards the trees.

She moved slowly. In the two months she had lived on the property, her daily walks had carved out a network of paths. Well-worn goat trails that circled the rear of the house taking her through dips and turns. Cutting lines through thick bush and grassy clearings. These excursions gave her the peace and solitude to enjoy the fading glory of spring while sorting through the images that shadowed her mind.

There was also another reason for the walks, one that was less about healing but pressing nevertheless. Lucy made her way to a fallen tree and bent with her fingers curling inside the husk of wood. She pulled out the packet and popped a cigarette in her mouth.

Some old habits were harder to shake off. She lit the smoke and blew out a white plume. Overhead, a kookaburra laughed, its cry more like a monkey's chatter than a bird song.

"It's not that funny." Lucy sucked in the smoke, savouring the thick tobacco taste. "It's the only one this week." Now she spoke to herself and not the bird. *God knows I need it.*

The email was from Detective Randal, one of the officers she'd spoken to while still in hospital. When the message landed in her inbox the night before, she couldn't bring herself to read it. The trial was approaching. Holsey's trial. He would be first, then later would come Ruth's turn in court. The email was the beginning of the final chapter. That's how Randal had worded it some months ago when giving her an update.

But was it the final chapter? Maybe for the police and courts, but not for her. Not for Tim. Lucy held the cigarette between her fingers, watching the tip glow. After being arrested, Holsey and Ruth had turned on each other, both claiming the other did the killing. They would both face a lengthy trial. For the victims, there was the torture of reliving every detail of the ordeal. And for Tim, who'd been held captive and tortured, it would mean hours, if not days, on the stand. His past would be thrown up for all the world to speculate over.

Lucy ground the end of the cigarette out and placed the butt in a small metal tin which she stowed with the packet in its hiding place. She held her hands out in front of her, fingers splayed. Steady, not so much as a quiver. *Progress.*

She picked up her pace on the walk back, her feet scrunching over the path. She'd read the email as soon as she reached the veranda. With the decision made, her shoulders straightened. Maybe the trials would bring closure. Maybe staring into Holsey's eyes and then Ruth's would give her some satisfaction. She hoped so because she had too much in her life to let the despicable pair hold her thoughts captive.

As she broke through the trees, the house came in sight and ahead of it a familiar figure. *He's back*. Lucy sped up, jogging the last thirty metres. With the email forgotten, she bounded into his arms.

"Miss me?" Damon lifted her off the ground and the both of them nearly toppled over.

Chuckling, he set her down. If he smelled the tobacco, he gave no indication. With his hands around her waist he kissed her, a long soft kiss that sent a spark of heat through her body.

She pulled back, off-balance and breathless from the run and the kiss. "You're a day early, not that I'm complaining."

"Well," he said, taking her hand and leading her onto the veranda. "Brock and I found the woman's husband. It turned out he was in Kalgoorlie, living it up with a friend of his nineteen-year-old daughter, a skimpy barmaid."

Lucy followed him into the house. "Sounds weird." She loved hearing about Damon's latest cases, but couldn't quite get her head around his new-found friendship with Brock. After things calmed down in Night Town, Brock resigned from the police force and went to work for Damon's old friend Larson Granger. It wasn't unusual for Damon and Brock to work on a security job or missing person case for Granger Investigations. She could understand Brock enjoying Damon's company. He was a magnetic person, at least she felt inexorably drawn to him.

Once in the kitchen Damon turned and kissed her again. This time the kiss was deeper and when they parted he ran his fingers down a strand of her hair that had tumbled loose when she jumped into his arms.

"How have you been?" She knew what the question meant. He wanted to know about the nightmares and bouts of shaking.

There was worry in his eyes and she desperately wanted to tell him she was fine. But lying to Damon was the one thing she'd promised never to do.

"I had an email about the trial." She took a step back and rubbed the side of her head at the sight of the old injury from when Holsey cracked her head against the car window. "At least I think it's about the trial." Sometimes she had headaches. Throbbing pain that the doctor said might now be more about post-traumatic stress than any physical problem. "It came yesterday, but I was going to open it when I got back from my walk." Damon nodded, maybe expecting her to say more.

Lucy opened the fridge and pulled out a jug of iced tea. Like with the cigarettes, she was trying to cut down on her coffee intake in the hope of reducing the shaking in her hands, although she suspected the periodic tremors were more about panic or stress than caffeine. "Tell me more about the case and the laconic Brock Day. How's he handling life outside the police force?" She was changing the subject and they both knew it. But Damon didn't push her on the email. That was one of the things she loved about him. He knew when to give her space.

Their relationship was still new. They hadn't talked about love, but in that moment Lucy knew she did indeed love this man. It wasn't a surprise but more like something she'd always known and now saw through fresh eyes.

The three of them, her, Tim, and Damon, were making something of their own on this beautiful patch of land. A family of sorts. And while she dreaded the trial, she knew it would come and go, but she'd finally found something solid, and that was enough. More than enough.

The End

If you enjoyed this book, please let others know by leaving a quick review on Amazon. Also, if you spot anything untoward in the paperback, get in touch. We strive for the best quality and appreciate reader feedback.

editor@thebookfolks.com

www.thebookfolks.com

The Sequels:

ANNA WILLETT

A KIDNAPPING, A MURDER, AND A WOMAN WHO WON'T GIVE IN

COLD VALLEY
NIGHTMARE

The Australian bush is unforgiving, so when a child goes missing Lucy does all she can to find him. But she'll enter into the affairs of a small town who don't like strangers. She'll be in severe danger if she further meddles in their business.

Available on Kindle and in paperback from Amazon.

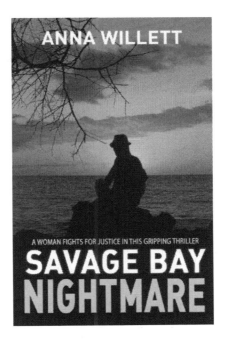

ANNA WILLETT

A WOMAN FIGHTS FOR JUSTICE IN THIS GRIPPING THRILLER

SAVAGE BAY NIGHTMARE

When journalist Lucy Hush's brother is accused of murder, she goes on a desperate search for the truth. But her inquiries are unwelcome and it's not long before she stirs up a vipers' nest full of subterfuge and deceit. Can she get justice for her brother, or will she become another victim?

Available on Kindle and in paperback from Amazon.

Also by Anna Willett:

BACKWOODS RIPPER
RETRIBUTION RIDGE
UNWELCOME GUESTS
FORGOTTEN CRIMES
CRUELTY'S DAUGHTER
VENGEANCE BLIND
THE WOMAN BEHIND HER

ANNA WILLETT

A GRIPPING ACTION SUSPENSE THRILLER

BACKWOODS
RIPPER

Paige and her husband Hal are on a babymoon, a romantic holiday before their child is born. When misfortune strikes and Hal is injured, they are left stranded in the wilderness. Paige finds two women who offer to help. But when they turn nasty, how far will she have to go to protect her unborn child?

Available on Kindle and in paperback from Amazon.

ANNA WILLETT

A DARK, GRIPPING AND INTENSE SUSPENSE THRILLER

RETRIBUTION
RIDGE

Milly assumes that her sister's invitation to go hiking in the Outback is to heal old wounds. A mutual friend joins them for the trek, and at first things seem to be going well. But a nasty surprise awaits Milly and she is thrown into a dangerous situation with a life or death choice over who and what is most important to her.

Available on Kindle and in paperback from Amazon.

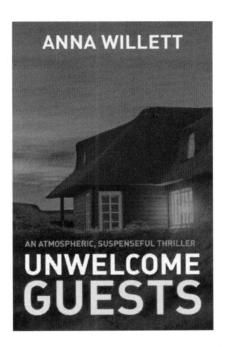

ANNA WILLETT

AN ATMOSPHERIC, SUSPENSEFUL THRILLER

UNWELCOME
GUESTS

Caitlin seeks to build bridges with her husband after the loss of their baby. Unfortunately, their holiday getaway is not what it seems when they find a man held hostage in the cellar. When the house owner turns up, armed and dangerous, Caitlin will have to quickly decide whom she should trust.

Available on Kindle and in paperback from Amazon.

ANNA WILLETT

A GRIPPING PSYCHOLOGICAL SUSPENSE THRILLER

FORGOTTEN
CRIMES

Gloria's reunion with a friend triggers disturbing flashbacks of events four years ago. She is encouraged to visit the place where a woman died. Gloria goes along to make sense of the strange memories that are re-emerging. But doing so will force her to confront an awful episode in her past.

Available on Kindle and in paperback from Amazon.

ANNA WILLETT

A RIVETING PSYCHOLOGICAL SUSPENSE THRILLER

CRUELTY'S
DAUGHTER

Mina's father was a brute and a thug. She got over him. Now another man wants to fill his shoes. Can Mina overcome the past and protect herself? 'Cruelty's Daughter' is about a woman who tackles her demons and takes it upon herself to turn the tables on a violent man.

Available on Kindle and in paperback from Amazon.

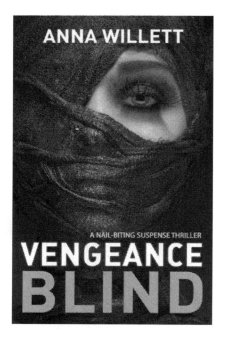

Of poor eyesight and confined to a wheelchair after a road accident, a successful author is alone in her house. She begins to hear strange noises, but is relieved when a care assistant arrives. However, her problems are only just beginning as she is left to the mercy of someone with a grudge to bear. The question for Belle is who, and why?

Available on Kindle and in paperback from Amazon.

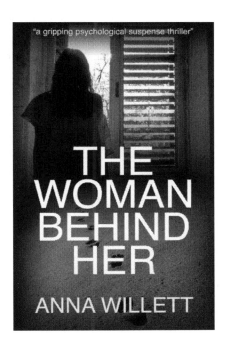

"a gripping psychological suspense thriller"

THE WOMAN BEHIND HER

ANNA WILLETT

When Jackie Winter inherits her aunt's house, she makes a chilling discovery. Worse, she finds that she is being watched. When someone is murdered nearby, she finds herself in the frame. Can she join up the dots and prove her innocence?

Available on Kindle and in paperback from Amazon.

Printed in Poland
by Amazon Fulfillment
Poland Sp. z o.o., Wrocław

59539225R00136